THE DRAGON KEEPER CHRONICLES

AZURAN

TAI MANIVONG

PRINT ISBN: 978-1-7325141-0-2

Editor: Developmental - Erin Young
Developmental review - Bryan Saliba
Copy Edit- Anna Solemani
Proofreading - Leonora Bulbeck

For Alyssa and Teya
Special thanks Dorothy Ross for beta reading Azuran

CRIMSON took in a deep breath, keeping her snout above the water as it slapped against her wiry red fur. Crimson was Norterridane, a fierce breed of dogs who had the ability to connect with and protect dragons. In protecting them, she had almost lost everything.

The memories of chaos and horror flooded her mind. The den tunnels collapsing, the serpents attacking her home, and her friend Midnight nearly dying from battle wounds was enough to make Crimson question everything in her life. Crimson had narrowly escaped death, and the Norterridane had just begun to rebuild the broken tunnels of their home. But now, just below the subtle currents of Crystal

Lake, a dragon was hatching. A new hope in a world in disarray.

Holding her breath, Crimson paddled down beneath the cool water toward the dragon egg. A small turquoise nose pushed its way through the crack in the eggshell. Piece by piece the egg broke apart and the shells floated away. The sea dragon emerged covered in smooth turquoise scales. Enlarged wings that mimicked those of a moth propelled the dragon through the water. Gills fluttered as the dragon swam up toward Crimson and rubbed her head against her fur.

A rush of cool and calm dragon power flowed between them. Crimson's stomach turned as the familiar pang of power-induced nausea hit her. Gills formed behind her button ears, near where the jawbone connected to her neck. She breathed in the cool lake water. The dragon magic connected them, as if they had known each other all of their lives. The instant connection surprised her at first, just like the time she first called fire from her claws. Crimson relaxed and let the magic take over calming her body. She hadn't expected gills. She would have loved a magical translucent shield that many dragon keepers created when they shared power. But gills gave Crimson a jolt of excitement at the prospect of being able to explore the depths of the lake, and the thoughts of battle faded away. The dragon snapped at a small minnow. Crimson swam after a silver scaled fish, caught it with her claws, and fed it to the dragon. She eagerly consumed it.

Crimson swam to the lakeshore and shook the water from her fur. The smell of dragon entered her nose. A musty lizard odor mixed with the slight sweetness of eucalyptus made the dragon scent unique from that of other reptilian creatures. Even with a highly developed sense of smell, the dragon scent overwhelmed all non-dragon smells. Crimson's head began to throb. Muddy soil covered the ground near the reeds, and she pushed the hatchling toward it. The dragon's oversized wings dragged through the mud. Crimson rubbed the mud from her paws onto the dragon's body, and she squawked in protest.

"You don't like the mud? It will keep you hidden," Crimson said. The dragon squawked again.

Crimson rubbed a pawful of mud on the dragon's back, and slowly the smells of the world returned. She had been lucky to discover that trick early as a dragon keeper.

"Almost done," Crimson said, looking affectionately at the dragon. The dragon rubbed her mud-covered head against Crimson's leg and looked up at her with purple eyes.

"Your eyes remind me of covellite. It's a stone in the lake. I want to name you Covelli."

The dragon's eyes beamed, and she brushed against Crimson again.

Crimson sniffed the air and looked around the reeds that grew at the lake's edge. The plants near the lake were tall enough to hide in. Farther south, the grass-covered hills peaked out above the reeds, and Jasperillian plants grew sporadically between the grasses. The dragon scent was hidden for now, but they would still need a suitable den. River weasels and cave lizards were often seen near Crystal Lake. The Jasperillian leaves had a powerful smell that helped mask the smell of dragons, but even their potent smell would eventually fade.

Crimson had never made a den. She had lived with her mother until she found the dragon eggs, and when she took care of her last dragons, she stayed with Midnight in his den. Midnight was her best friend, a warrior and dragon keeper. He had taught her everything she knew about dragon keeping. He had been injured by Azuran in the serpent battle, trying to protect her. She knew the basics of den making, and the chances of finding such a readily available shelter here on the southeastern side of the lake were slim. Crimson searched the reeds for a suitable place. Small hills stood a short distance away from the lake. Crimson walked to the hill and scratched the dirt. The dirt was drier than expected. Crimson dug with her front paws, moving dirt out of the way. As she moved the dirt away, more fell from above. Crimson backed out of the small hole and groaned. This wouldn't work, and there were no trees or bushes. Roots would have helped support the ceiling. Crimson sighed and looked at Covelli. The dragon had found a snail to play with and pawed at it whenever its head poked out of the shell.

A light breeze blew from across the lake, shaking the reeds and causing ripples across the water. Crimson sniffed. The scent of an older dragon came from upwind, weak and less sweet, and a slight smell of something else: serpent.

The reeds rustled and cracked. Whatever it was, it was moving fast. She couldn't smell it clearly. She couldn't see it. Crimson stood alert and growled. Dragon scales rubbed against her back leg. Crimson glanced down. Covelli stood between her legs, almost blending in with the mud around her, staring up at the reeds, trembling.

A black dragon head appeared from within the

reeds. Like a giant snake, its head moved from side to side. Smooth, shiny black scales covered its body, and sharp ridges covered its spine. Three spines stuck up over the ears on each side, and it turned its eyes inquisitively upon Crimson. The blue eyes, threatening and beautiful all at once, and very familiar.

"Azuran?" Crimson gasped. The last time she had seen him had been in battle, when he had attacked Midnight and the other Norterridane. The hardest thing to process about the battle was seeing Azuran. She couldn't believe it. He had been her first dragon. She had protected him as a hatchling, until a serpent came and tried to kill them. Azuran had fallen into the swift currents of the Sapphire River and over the waterfall. He had died, or so she had believed, until he showed up fighting with the enemy. He fled shortly after she saw him, when more dragons came to the aid of the Norterridane.

Now he stood before her, majestic yet terrifying. His large head moved closer to her. She wasn't sure if she should run or try to fight.

"You're far from home," Azuran said, his voice even. His mouth was so close to Crimson that she could feel his breath on her fur. His head was a least three times as large as Crimson's small body.

Crimson took a step back, trying to remain calm. She could call the dragon fire from her claws. A rare ability she had gained when she first found Azuran and his sister's eggs. But it wouldn't hurt him. He was an Obsidian dragon. He had impenetrable scales. Scales that were invincible to everything, except other Obsidian dragon claws. He could easily kill her, but something told her he would have already killed her if he wanted to. His eyes didn't seem threatening like they had on the battlefield. He wanted something else.

"Do you remember me?" Crimson said, forcing herself to stand tall. Covelli's tail wrapped tightly around her leg, willing her to stay put.

"I remember how you stopped me in battle, with that arc of fire. It brought back many fractured memories. It seems you have mastered your power well," Azuran said.

Azuran had killed several Norterridane and was about to kill Midnight when Crimson intervened, calling a wall of fire from her claws. When the Schorl serpents had attacked the city in an attempt to capture dragon hatchlings and to gain their power, the Norterridane had fought them off with the help of dragon-kind. Crimson had called upon the power of all the nearby dragons and created a shield of fire that incinerated the nearby serpents, hastening their retreat. Crimson didn't understand why she could channel the power of many dragons and had only been able to do so with the help of a mysterious white Norterridane named Jasper. Crimson was still learning how to call on her seemingly innate powers and doubted that she could call that much power again on her own.

The scent of serpent was stronger now and coming from Azuran. He had lived with them so long their scent must have stayed with him.

"You smell of serpent," Crimson said, sharper than she intended. "Are they still here in Genorrdia?"

Azuran's expression changed for a brief second, then hardened. It seemed like a topic he was reluctant to talk about. Then he shook his head. "I am not sure; Onixian and I were separated."

"Is that the serpent's name?"

Azuran looked down and saw Covelli for the first time. "Another dragon!"

Azuran's muscles jerked, as if he was going to jump off the ground, but he relaxed his body and he moved his head toward Covelli, who squeaked and backed away.

"I won't hurt you," he said.

Then the dragons were silent. Covelli moved closer to Azuran, and their noses touched for just a moment. Azuran's blue eyes looked tenderly on his kin.

It seemed so peaceful, but his enormous head and large dragon teeth reminded Crimson of the danger she was most likely in. How could she be so calm when he had almost killed Midnight and Torbern? Could it be that she was still thinking of him as a dragon hatchling instead of this dangerous beast before her?

"I have not heard dragon thoughts in such a long time." Azuran sighed as if he had longed for it. Longed for a connection. Dragons could converse in their own telepathic language, even inside their eggs. Azuran and his twin sister, Chalcedony, had communicated this way before they learned to speak Norterridane to communicate with Crimson.

Azuran lay down, stretching his body out among the reeds, flattening them into the ground. His large tail, which looked like a braided black root, curled around his body. A whip tail that could cause serious damage to anything attacking him.

Crimson shook her head. "What are you doing here?"

"This is my home."

"Dragons are supposed to live on Alannador. Don't you want to reunite with the dragons?"

"The serpents are my kind now," Azuran said, pawing playfully with Covelli. The little mud-covered dragon swiped at Azuran's claws, and he knocked her over gently. "I am sure I'll find them eventually."

Covelli jumped toward Azuran's muzzle, tripped on her wings, and tumbled over. Crimson watched them, wondering why Azuran hadn't gone to Alannador, like the other mature dragons. She had to find out more. Did he really feel like one of them?

Azuran didn't know if the serpents had left, but this was Crimson's chance to convince him to find his kind. He couldn't go looking for the serpents, or they would have an Obsidian dragon as an enemy, and that would be unthinkable.

"Didn't you hear the call?" Crimson said. "Didn't you want to go home?"

"The call?"

"The call all dragons hear when they mature, calling them home to Alannador. Chalcedony called it a melody." Crimson hummed the peaceful yet sad song that Chalcedony had sang when the Obsidian dragons turned the dead to ashes with their fire and sent their kin to the afterlife.

"I heard something like that, once or twice, but I did not understand what it was. Onixian told me to ignore it."

To hear the call and not go—what does that mean for a dragon? Has he abandoned his kind forever? Maybe I could help him reconnect with them. Can I still feel for his power, as I can other dragons?

Crimson relaxed as much as she could in his presence. Still on edge, she let her mind drift through the air. She focused on his heartbeat, like she had when he was young. The rhythmic thumping focused her thoughts. She called for his power, concentrating on the feeling she had when she'd first connected with him. The joy and comfort she had felt at that moment rushed back into her mind. His power came to her like the hot rays of the sun heating the rocks upon the shore.

Small flames of white lit up her claw, different from the blue fire that now came without the aid of dragons. The power that connected keeper and dragon. It was weaker than before, much weaker than her bond with Covelli, but it was there, the heat merely a glimmer of the warmth it had been. The emotion that came from the connection was unexpected, and a tear rolled down her furry cheek.

Azuran moved back in surprise, but not from the flames. Crimson knew he had felt it too. The connection was overwhelming. The expression on

Azuran's face was one of confusion and possibly fear. He backed away.

Wind blew in from the north, and with it, the scents of two approaching warriors.

Azuran growled and snapped his tail, sending several reeds flying.

"No, Azuran," Crimson said.

Azuran turned away from Covelli and leapt into the air, flying low over the hills toward the eastern Black Mountain range. Crimson watched until he was a small speck in the sky. She longed to go back in time and save him, to make up for lost time. Wherever he was going, she had to find him; she had to get him back.

Covelli, eyes wide, stared into the sky where Azuran had flown. Her scales shimmered in the light. Crimson wondered what Azuran had said to her, but she was too young to speak Norterridane. Azuran didn't seem like an evil monster, like the serpents. In fact, when they had connected, he seemed almost sad.

"He was playful," Crimson said. "I didn't expect that."

Two Norterridane came through the reeds: Beryl, chief guard, a medium-brown Norterridane, and an unfamiliar tricolored male. Beryl had been Crimson's warrior trainer. She remembered clearly his disappointment in how well she had progressed. Her training as a warrior had ceased when she found two dragon eggs. After the serpent battle, Beryl had sent Crimson to the lake's edge to find the dragon's egg as a sign he finally had accepted her as a keeper.

"Crimson," Beryl said as he emerged, pushing his nose up in greeting, "I am glad to see the dragon has hatched. There is another dragon scent here. What is it?"

"It was Azuran."

Beryl's fur prickled. "What did he want?"

"I am not sure," Crimson said. She recounted their exchange.

"The Elders will want to know of this," Beryl said. "Have you bonded with the hatchling?"

"Yes," Crimson said, calling upon the cool, calm power. The gills reformed on her neck.

"This is Labrad," Beryl said, gesturing behind him. The tricolor Norterridane of white, black, and brown stepped further out of the reeds. The dark brown fur on his face looked like a mask. The drastic contrast in color highlighted his blue eyes, a rare color for Norterridane. "He is a dragon keeper."

"What is this about?" Crimson said.

"The Elders have summoned you," Labrad said, his voice calm and confident. "They want to speak with you immediately, about the powerful wall of fire you created during the battle."

"We need to leave at once," Beryl said. He observed the dragon carefully as if he was deciding what do with her. "Will she follow you?"

Crimson followed his gaze down at the hatchling. Bright purple eyes looked back. "Yes, she will. Covelli, let's go for a swim."

Covelli needed no prodding. She followed Crimson through the muddy reeds and splashed into the lake.

CHAPTER 2

OVELLI swam gracefully underwater. Her oversized wings helped her move effortlessly through the lake. It seemed like she was flying. Her legs were motionless by her side, and her tail moved back and forth to help her change directions.

Crimson swam after her, trying to catch up. She reached for the dragon power. The cool, breezy wave of Covelli's dragon magic flowed through her mind and body. Crimson felt the water flow through her nose and out the magic-enhanced gills. She pushed herself through the water with her paws, delighting in the feeling. Fish darted out of the way as she swam.

Crimson spent much of her time in water, as most Norterridane did. They were fish hunters, and she could hold her breath for quite a long time. But feeling the water flow through her dragon-enhanced gills gave her a sense of freedom to explore the underwater world that she never had before.

Broad-leaved pondweed, eelgrass, and Jasperillian grew sporadically along the upper layer of the lake, creating a green expanse for fish and other lake animals to hide. Farther down the bank, the plants receded, and the water cooled. At the bottom of the lake was something large and dark that spread across the lake bottom like three enormous claw marks.

Crimson swam to the surface, catching up to Beryl, who had been taking turns with Labrad surfacing for air and keeping an eye on Crimson and Covelli. "There is something under the lake. It looks like dark slashes in the dirt."

"It's a large crevasse, nothing down there but darkness."

"Someone's explored it?"

"The Magi investigated it long ago, before even I was born."

The Magi were those Norterridane who were born with the ability to use magic. They did not need to keep dragons to have power, but they only used their magic for healing and bettering the lives of the Norterridane.

"I think it would be really neat to see."

Beryl swam close to Crimson. "Just make sure your first duty is to your dragon."

And once again she was back to being treated like a pup.

Crimson swam back under the water. The sooner she met with the Elders, the sooner she could get back to raising Covelli on her own, and she could explore where she wanted.

"Come on, Covelli," Crimson barked, though her words were muffled underwater. Covelli's ears twitched at the sound.

Crimson and Covelli followed Beryl deeper into Crystal Lake, to an underwater tunnel. The tunnel turned upward and above the water level, branching off into several dens and passageways. Large boulders stood on both sides of the newly opened entrance, which had been sealed during the serpent attack. The Underground dens had been crafted in the hills and rocky slopes of the Black Mountains. The passage split into sections, leading to the upper and lower corridors of the city.

Crimson covered Covelli with mud once again, and the scent of heated fish filled the tunnel. The fish-drying caves were somewhere under the city, close by, though Crimson had never seen them. Covelli smelled the air and squawked.

"She is hungry," Labrad said.

"I will get her a fish; I will meet you at the Elders' cave," Beryl said, and disappeared through a tunnel on the left toward the fish-drying caves. Beryl left so quickly Crimson didn't have time to say that she had already fed her. Covelli was probably just interested in the smell. She shrugged and watched Covelli's awkward walking. On land, Covelli was not graceful. Her wings were large for her size, and she stepped on them often as she walked through the tunnel. Her tail had a large forked fin on the end. A long top fin curved downward over the short, triangle-shaped lower fin and dragged on the ground.

"Pick up your wings, Covelli," Crimson said, and the dragon tried her best to hold them up on her back. It was a struggle.

"She will get stronger," Labrad said. "Sea dragons spend most of their hatchling life in water, building up their muscle strength."

"Can they fly?" Crimson asked, suddenly wondering how Covelli would be able to with such heavy wings.

"They can fly, but they don't often—they live in

the oceans and spend very little time on land or in the sky."

The walk to the Elders' cave is going to be a long one. Crimson sighed and walked near Covelli, encouraging her.

"Did you keep a sea dragon?" she asked Labrad.

"Yes, several. Though my latest dragon was a sand dragon. I called him Smokey."

"Several sea dragons. Have you ever seen what's in the crevasse?"

"Ya know, I haven't," Labrad said. "I took my dragons to my keeper den near the Sapphire River. Just always kept my dragons there."

"A keeper den?"

"You have to find your own place where you want to keep your dragons, and make a den there. Once you have a good idea of where you feel the most comfortable."

"I guess I still have some things to learn," Crimson said.

"You didn't have much dragon training, so don't be hard on yourself."

The group walked along a dark tunnel lit up with glow stones, stones that absorbed sunlight and shone almost as bright. The Underground was in the middle of the vast Black Mountain range, partly hidden in the foothills and surrounded by redwood forest. It had many entrances, some through the forest or the mountains, but dragon keepers were only allowed to enter through certain tunnels that young Norterridane pups did not visit. Crimson remembered the off-limits tunnels when she was a pup. She had even caught the scent of a dragon but had never been allowed to see one. Her mother had said it was to keep pups from running off, looking for dragon eggs and being attacked by cave lizards.

There were many tunnels now, some slanting downward, others curving this way and that. The ones built deeper into the earth were stone, while the passages moving upward were dirt mixed with stone. Every den had more than one exit so that they could escape if needed.

The scents of Norterridane became more abundant, but none of them Crimson recognized.

"These tunnels were once full of dragon keepers. That is, back when it all first started," Labrad said, "before we knew their scent attracted cave lizards."

"Until the lake swelled and the tunnels flooded," Crimson added.

"Yes, that is true. One of these dens belonged to Jasper."

"Jasper?"

"Yes, she was one of the first dragon keepers and a Magi."

Jasper was female? Crimson thought. She had heard of Jasper, the greatest dragon keeper of all time, but she had always assumed she would be male, like so many others.

"I've heard that Jasper was able to share dragon power, like I can," Crimson said, looking behind her to make sure Covelli was still following. She slowed her pace a bit. One of Covelli's claws was hooked in her wing again. It took her a minute to unhook it. She squawked happily when she was free.

"I wonder what is taking Beryl so long with that fish," Labrad said.

The glow stones of the main hall came into view. Covelli walked slower now, taking in the sight. There was nothing like it. Crimson remembered the first time she had seen it as a pup; she had never wanted to stop looking at the sparkling stones. There were hundreds of them, lining the walls of the cavern and lighting up the darkness like daylight. The cavern was empty now, but hundreds of Norterridane would gather here for meetings and celebrations. Pups were trained in other parts of the Underground, in the higher levels, to become warriors, Magi, hunters, explorers, and other jobs needed in the Underground.

"Come on, Covelli," Crimson said, and nudged the dragon toward the long tunnel that led to the Elders' cave. She heard a voice coming from a nearby den.

"Congratulations! You have been chosen to be dragon keepers. It is a big responsibility, and not one to be taken lightly. You will have the life of another in your hands, and it is your duty to raise and protect your dragon."

Only the best Norterridane of each class became dragon keepers. Crimson knew that if she hadn't accidentally found those two Obsidian dragon eggs and bonded with them, she would not have been chosen as a keeper. She had not been the best warrior, and it had only been luck that she had found dragon eggs.

Labrad peeked in the den as he walked by, looking at all the new keepers with pride. Crimson glanced in too as they walked by. The new keepers were all about the same age as Crimson; she had become one much younger than usual. Closest to the den entrance was a small brown Norterridane, his eyes wide and sucking in all the heroic ideas of being a dragon keeper.

The trainees turned at the scent of the dragon, and

the trainer hurried to the den entrance to block them from coming out to investigate.

"And that," the trainer said, "that is your first smell of a dragon hatchling. Please let the dragon pass without disturbance."

The Norterridane stared in awe as the hatchling walked past. Then they looked at Crimson, and their eyes widened even more.

"My apologies," Labrad said, hurrying Crimson and Covelli along. "We will take the east tunnels on the way back."

The trainer nodded and continued. "While we see it as an honor to protect dragon young, we must also protect our way of life. The many jobs of the city are important, from fish hunter to warrior. When you are granted a dragon, you will be taken away from the city to live and guard the dragon on your own. This is what you have been trained to do. Yes, it is dangerous, but with the shared dragon magic, you can succeed."

"They seemed more surprised to see me than a dragon," Crimson said.

"It is not every day that they see the red Norterridane who called a wall of white fire. You're quite a legend."

"But how did they know? They weren't there."

"News travels fast, and your color is unique, just like your abilities, it would seem," Labrad said as several other Norterridane came out of their dens, smelling dragon scent. When they saw Crimson, they stared and whispered amongst each other. Crimson hurried Covelli along, hoping this meeting would end soon and she would be away from all the prying eyes.

CHAPTER 3

MALACHITE, the serpent king, stood on the edge of the aspen forest, still like stone, as a black dragon flew overhead. The dragon was searching, but it wouldn't find him, nor the other serpents hidden in the forest. Obsidian dragons did not have the best sense of smell, and the wind blew down from above the cliffs, across the forest, sending any smells toward the eastern ocean. Malachite's gray scales partially blended in with the grayish bark of the aspen trees, and the dense forest spread over hundreds of miles, taking up the southern half of the continent of Genorrdia. A small bird landed on the tip of Malachite's wing. The stillness of the serpent, perfected with years of practice, made him appear to be part of his environment. In seconds, he snapped his top arm up and snatched the bird, squeezing the life from it before throwing it in his mouth and gulping it down.

Only his red-tipped tusks could have given him away. The powerful magic from the melted crystalline sardonyx stone clung to his tusks like sap on a tree, giving him great power. The crystalline sardonyx was a rare and powerful stone that Obsidian dragons could chew to create a hot fire that would turn enemies to ashes. Serpents could not chew it, but Malachite had found melted stone and affixed it to his tusks and claws. With it, he had the power to kill Obsidian dragons.

Malachite scanned the forest. One by one, shapes began to move. The Schorl came to life. Where the strangely shaped trees and branches had been now stood large dragon-like creatures, with six arms, bat-like wings, and tusks. Muscular legs held massive bodies, long, scaled tails twitched, and necks cracked as the serpents stretched their bodies, awaiting their leader's orders. It was said that dragons and serpents were once the same species, separated by dark magic. Malachite could appreciate the similarities, but dragons, save the Obsidians, were much weaker.

"The dragon has once again searched the forest," Malachite said. "You have stayed hidden well these last months, and we must continue to do so, but we cannot stay here in the forest forever. The stone-reader will have the answers."

The serpents nodded.

"Fairburn," Malachite called. The stone-reader moved by his side. She alone could read and find magic stones. Her gray-keeled scales reflected the sun. They were a mix of soft charcoal and light gray, creating diamond patterns along her back and tail. Her tusks were also gray, and shorter than those of the male serpents.

"What do the stones tell you?" Malachite said quietly, so only a few could hear.

Fairburn's red eyes focused intently on the magic stones in her claws.

"The small bit of sardonyx was all this land had; there are other magic stones, but none as powerful as the sardonyx."

"We cannot possibly win this war without more."

"There are still magic stones in the wasteland to the east; these could ward off the hunger if we find them. But near the Norterridane city, there is something powerful. I am not sure what it is. I sensed it when I first came to Genorrdia, I thought it was the crystalline sardonyx, but it is something else. Something in the lake, deep within. I thought it could be the magic of dragons, but this magic is different; I can see that now."

"Something to investigate …" Malachite began.

A serpent stepped up to the king. "We have already lost a battle with the Norterridane. Perhaps we should not risk another. We are better off raiding Alannador, as we always have before."

"We planned the last battle foolishly; I will not make that mistake again." Malachite turned to Fairburn. "Is it powerful, this magic you sense?"

"Yes, very." Fairburn looked him in the eye.

"Then if it is powerful, it is worth investigating," Malachite said. "Andalus, how are the Schorl? Do they grow restless?"

Andalus, the lead scout and a highly respected Schorl, was one of Malachite's most trusted allies. He was the largest of the Schorl, and one of two with whom Malachite had shared the crystalline sardonyx power.

"They're always restless. They question your decision to stay here, and wonder why we do not return to Calimdural," Andalus said.

"There is nothing for us on that barren continent, nothing but death. If we did not kill each other, we would have died sooner or later. Remember Calaver? He was a great leader who rose above the hunger and led the serpents to an era of greatness. Remember how the dragons feared us? That is what I want for Schorl. I am stronger now than I have ever been, and stronger than any other serpent. But it is not enough for just me. I need to empower all serpents. Just as I have empowered you."

Andalus glanced around the forest at the serpents. "What you want is a dream. The curse is too strong."

"Calaver believed the curse could be cured," Fairburn said, interrupting. She moved her claw along the stone and looked off in the distance at the seemingly endless sea of trees. "We need to get—"

"This is not a curse. Craving magic and taking it from dragons is a blessing. A blessing that has made me powerful. It has made us powerful. Any Schorl that says otherwise is weak."

Malachite followed her gaze across the forest to a vast plain of grass. This home had been a temporary solution when the dragons had come in aid of the Norterridane. The aspen turned out to be a fine hiding place, especially at night. The plan had been simple: attack the Norterridane and take the baby dragons, but there was no way that Malachite could kill so many Obsidians in an open battle.

He had to be smarter. There were two left, and if

he was clever, he would be able to get rid of them both.

"You were right to leave the hatchlings on Xenoti," Fairburn said.

"I know. The dragons would not have believed that we had fled if we had kept them. Besides, they did not bond with us as Azuran had with Onixian." He raised his dominant hand and pointed with a red-tipped claw to the looming Black Mountains in the distance. Each time he looked at his hands and tusks, he remembered how he had found the molten crystalline sardonyx. They had searched for it for years, and by luck Fairburn and Onixian had found Genorrdia, and the volcano Mount Xenoti. Inside the volcano was a small pool of melted sardonyx. A brave serpent guard, Zircon, had tried to drink it to retrieve the magic, but surprisingly, he had died, poisoned by the stone. Malachite had carefully dipped his claws in the hot red liquid, not knowing for sure what would happen. He felt the power of the sardonyx flow through his claws and into his body, giving him a strength like no other. Malachite and Andalus quickly covered their tusks in the molten stone. The sardonyx-tipped tusks could penetrate the Obsidian dragon skin. Malachite had tested it on the dragon Azuran and it had worked. Then, during the battle, he killed an

Obsidian, and, oh, what power he had felt. He could still feel the dragon magic flowing through his veins, quelling the hunger for magic and allowing him to think clearly.

"What of the mountains to the north?" Andalus said, pointing to the snowcapped mountains far beyond Xenoti.

Fairburn turned the glowing stone over in her hand and carved a small rune into the coarse, grainy surface. The rune glowed a pale yellow. "Yes, they could provide a temporary haven."

"Why the mountains?" Malachite said.

"Our scales will blend in with the landscape. There is an abundance of grey slate. Perhaps we will not have to be so fearful of the Obsidian dragons there."

"You may be right. Go and see what you can find out—"

"No," Fairburn interrupted. "We should all go. It will take days for him to return. The Obsidian dragon draws closer each time he searches. There are too many of us to go unnoticed forever."

"I will heed your advice, stone-reader." He turned to the serpents. "We will leave for the mountains when the sun sets. Hesson will lead the Schorl through the wasteland. Andalus and I will scout near the lake. I want to find out more about this mysterious power."

Fairburn nodded, and when the last rays of twilight began to disappear, the serpents left the forest.

CHAPTER 4

OICES could be heard down the tunnel, from the Elders' cave.

"We cannot afford to have an Obsidian dragon as an enemy. Send scouts; see what we can find out."

"Perhaps he can be persuaded to rejoin his kind."

Crimson and Labrad stepped into the Elders' cave. Beryl stood near the Elders. A dried fish lay at his paws.

"So, you decided to beat us here?" Labrad said playfully.

"Someone had to fill them in about Azuran," Beryl said. He bit the dried fish and dropped it near the young dragon. Covelli sank her teeth into it and gobbled down a chunk of fish meat and scales.

A few members of the Elder Council were

present. Crimson recognized two of them—Ferruginous, the High Elder, who made all final decisions, and Tourmaline, Crimson's mother and the newest member of the council. Two unfamiliar Norterridane, a white-and-black-gray female and a dark brindle female who pawed at two stones in the dirt, stood nearby. Covelli eating peacefully at her heels made Crimson feel slightly more comfortable, but her legs were shaking.

"Make yourself at ease," Ferruginous said in a commanding but somehow friendly tone. He had long silver fur partly covering his piercing gray eyes. Long nails on his paws, grown out from little use, pressed into the den floor.

Crimson sat down several paw lengths away, hoping to calm the uneasiness inside her.

The dark brindle lifted the stones in her mouth and dropped them near Crimson's feet. One of them glowed slightly.

Ferruginous turned to Crimson. "Identify these for me, please."

Crimson easily recognized basalt and shale. *Why is he testing my stone recognition?* They must have been looking for something specific. She looked at her mother for a hint. Tourmaline sat tall and proud. Her ears were erect, listening intently, and she showed no signs that she would help. Her role as an Elder trumped her role as mother, that much Crimson could tell, as it should. The Elders made decisions in the best interest of all Norterridane.

She looked down at the stones again, feeling the weight of the council members watching her. The specimen of basalt had a pale glow, barely recognizable, but she remembered how some rocks shimmered in different light. She sniffed it, smelling the minerals within.

"This one," Crimson said, patting the fine-grained, dark stone with her paw, "looks like a sedimentary stone. I can see the grooves inside of it." She recalled the lessons on stone identification she'd had as a pup. Identifying stones could keep one from getting lost, especially in winter, when scents were covered with snow. It also helped if you needed to find herbs that only grew in certain types of minerals.

"Anything else?" Ferruginous said.

"I believe this stone is shale, and this other one is basalt."

"Is that all you notice?"

"The basalt reminds me of a magic stone I noticed in Galena's den, nearly void of magic."

Crimson had met Galena after Azuran had fallen over the waterfall. Galena was a Magi who had helped Crimson and Chalcedony find a new home that was safe from the serpents. It was partly because of Galena that Chalcedony had survived.

"Just as I thought," Ferruginous said, and the others nodded. "Only Magi can sense magic in stones. No one else can see it."

Crimson's tail, which had been swishing on the cave floor, stopped moving. Her eyes widened and her legs stiffened. Her jaw fell open and a small whimper escaped. She must have heard wrong. *A Magi?*

Crimson regained her composure, shook her head, and perked her ears. Galena had been right, and this was a test.

"What does this mean?" Beryl said.

"It means she has the ability to draw power from other sources, not just stone."

"Just like Jasper," the white-and-gray Norterridane said.

"Yes, Lazuli," Ferruginous said. "Like Jasper."

The mood of the room darkened. Crimson took a step back and looked at the others. They all had questioning looks upon their faces.

Covelli moved under Crimson's front leg to hide from the stares.

Beryl spoke to Ferruginous. "How is this

possible? Magi are identified at birth. Wouldn't we have known?"

"Beryl, do you remember that Crimson seemed delayed in her warrior training? You said she was showing submissive behaviors when she should not have been," Tourmaline said.

"And then we put her in warrior training at Bowen's request," Beryl said.

"Perhaps she was delayed in the development of her Magi abilities," Tourmaline said.

Crimson's head was spinning. "I'm Magi?"

"It seems so. Your father, Bowen, must have kept you from your true destiny by insisting you become a warrior and a dragon keeper," Beryl growled.

He had not been fond of the idea of her becoming a warrior and never had missed the opportunity to express that opinion, even though he was the one to tell her where to find Covelli's egg, effectively accepting her as a keeper.

"Magi copy the first power they use. You first used Obsidian dragon fire, and thus that became your innate Magi ability. Since the days of Jasper, we have identified Magi early and train them in the healing arts. The first ability they learn is healing, and it becomes their instinctive magic. Magi have the ability to heal themselves without stones, a very useful ability. Jasper did not have that ability, and now neither do you."

"What does that mean for me?" Crimson asked.

"Obsidian fire has replaced the innate healing magic. But it will not stop your training."

"Dragon-keeper training?" Labrad said.

"No. She will be trained as a Magi. Which may be difficult as a dragon keeper," Ferruginous said. He nodded and the dark brindle came forward. "This is Amber. She is a Magi and will conduct your training, but first, do you know how you called the white-fire shield during the battle?"

"Yes," Crimson said, recalling that day. She had sensed all the dragons nearby and drawn on their magic. "I called on the powers of all the dragons around me. It was their power that created the fire."

"I see," he said. He turned to Amber and whispered into her ear. They conversed for a moment. He took a long breath.

"Hornblende, the king of dragons, noticed that as well. His energy drained with your pull of power. In another moment, he wouldn't have been able to stay in the air. He said it took all his strength to appear unaffected."

A large gust of wind blew into the Elder cave from the cliff exit. Green scales materialized as if out of thin air, and dragon claws set down a black Norterridane. Bowen walked into the cave, dipping his head low in respect to the Elders.

Crimson felt hot, and not dragon-power hot. Ear-twitching, wanting-to-run, panicky hot. Her tail twitched uneasily. Her paws felt heavy. What would her father think of what she had become? She stood still in awkward silence, awaiting his judgment.

CHAPTER 5

THE enormous forest dragon lay on a cliff ledge near the opening. Its tail tapped against the stone, and it moved its head through the den opening, eyes narrowed, studying Crimson for a moment. The dragon's green scaled head blocked most of the natural light as it moved farther into the den. Covelli hid behind Crimson's legs, seemingly in awe of the majestic beast. The forest dragon studied her with large green eyes, but it did not speak.

"This is Olivine," Bowen said, stepping forward to greet Crimson. "My, you have grown." He rubbed his head against hers for a brief moment. "Forgive me, Ferruginous. I had not expected my daughter to be in the Elder's cave. I have come with news. Should I address the council now?"

"We have important …"

Ferruginous's reply faded to a mumble as Crimson watched Olivine. The dragon's green eyes blended in with her scales, but the black catlike pupils gave her a sinister look. Crimson was mesmerized by the dragon, and then, almost unconsciously, Crimson summoned her power. A wave of heat filled her mind and radiated through her body. The cold chill of Covelli's power rippled through her veins and blended with the heat of the forest dragon's power. Olivine turned her gaze sharply on her. Heat from her nostrils flooded over Crimson's body.

"Enough!" the dragon roared, and both powers vanished.

"Olivine," Bowen said to the dragon, "what happened?"

"The young keeper called my power."

"I … I am sorry," Crimson said. "It just happened."

"And that is why you are here," the Elder said. "For the past week, we have been discussing how you were able to call upon the power of the dragons. The council wants to be cautious. We do not want you to be a danger to the Underground."

A danger? How could I be a danger?

As if reading her mind, Labrad spoke. "We have

never before seen power like yours; not since the time of Jasper, and her powers did not affect dragons in the same way. It seems that while she shared the dragons' power, you pull it from them, temporarily weakening them."

"I felt it too," Olivine said. "And I feel weaker even now. She pulled my power like wind carrying scent from prey. This pup did not even realize how easily she did it."

Ferruginous nodded and said, "This is what we feared. Crimson, you possess Magi abilities, but without training, it will be difficult to use the magic properly. Instead of sharing the power of just your hatchling, you are taking it from all dragons, weakening them temporarily, possibly even permanently. We do not know the extent. What happened after you called the wall of fire in the battle?"

"After the fire, I collapsed," said Crimson. "It was as if all the strength had been pulled from my body."

"Yes, using magic is weakening. You are lucky that much power did not kill you. You must learn how to use it wisely," Ferruginous said. He turned to Amber. "You will take over Magi training. Work with Crimson on learning basic magic skills and controlling her power."

Amber nodded.

"We must talk about how dragon keeping is changing," Ferruginous said to the council. "Before the serpents came, keepers would live alone with their dragons. It seemed the safest way, since we all know dragon scent attracts cave lizards. Then, if one dragon was killed, the Underground would not be in danger. This may not be true now, because the serpents know that the dragons hatch here. It's not a matter of *if* the serpents return. They *will* return, and we have to be ready."

"There have been no signs of the serpents," Beryl said. "Jet has scouted for days. But we still must be cautious. We may have to think about dragon keeping in packs."

"Jet?" Crimson said, barely above a whisper.

Ferruginous turned to Crimson. "Jet is one of the Obsidian dragons who stayed to make sure the serpents have retreated. I know this is a lot for you to take in. There is one more thing, and maybe the most important." He paused and looked around the room. "You cannot be a dragon keeper and a Magi. Once Covelli flies to Alannador, you will be only a Magi."

"Why?" Crimson blurted. The Elders turned their heads sharply, and Crimson tucked her tail between her legs. "My apologies."

Ferruginous continued. "Dragon magic and Magi magic do not mix well. There could be horrible consequences if this were to happen. The archives warn against it."

Mixing magic was what created the dragon plague. Crimson remembered Midnight had told her that when they had first met.

"Is there a way to be just a dragon keeper?" Tourmaline said, looking tenderly at Crimson. Bowen still did not say a word but looked up at Olivine. The dragon turned her head and brushed it against his fur.

"It would be possible if she could refrain from using Magi magic, but that will be difficult for such a young Norterridane. And she will be far more valuable to the Underground as a Magi," Ferruginous said.

"What are your orders, Ferruginous?" Beryl asked.

"When the dragon flies to Alannador, Crimson will move to the Magi den and continue training as a Magi."

"I can't be a dragon keeper?" Crimson said. It was her dream. It was her father's dream, and now they were going to take it away. She studied Bowen's face. He stood still and did not interrupt. There was no readable emotion. *Did he care at all?*

"Crimson, this is serious," Beryl said, "Imagine what could have happened if the serpents had not retreated. The dragons would have been weakened and unable to sustain the battle; the serpents could have won. Or worse, you may not have been able to control the fire, and many Norterridane could have died."

"You are not to use Magi magic, except under the direct supervision of Amber," Ferruginous said.

Tourmaline shook her head. "Then how will she protect her dragon?"

"She still has the ability to call fire from her claws without using power from other dragons. Let us not forget she survived on her own protecting two Obsidian dragons with hardly any training. She can protect the dragon with that. If you feel she is incompetent as a keeper, assign a warrior to stay with them."

After a moment, he added, "Or you can take the dragon and assign it to a new keeper."

"Is that possible?" Tourmaline said.

"Yes, but the ability is rare. Midnight was able to use Chalcedony's dragon magic, because Crimson does not share the power as other keepers do."

Covelli squawked. She backed up toward her

keeper defensively, tail whipping from side to side in defense.

"No, no, she is already attached," Labrad said. "The dragon needs to keep that bond."

"If she believes it is necessary, I will send a—" Beryl began.

Crimson shook her head; she knew what he was thinking. He wanted to send warriors to keep guard.

"I am certain she will be all right," Beryl added quickly.

Then Bowen's coarse voice stood out among the Elders. "She has proven herself as a keeper, and by right she should be allowed to keep this dragon. There are more important things the council must be aware of. If we could conclude this business with Crimson."

"What is so bad about using dragon magic?" Crimson dared to ask.

Olivine snorted, and hot breath filled the cave. "It is not yours to use."

Crimson backed away. There was venom in her voice. How much had she affected the dragons when she summoned their magic that day in battle?

Amber moved forward. "Adult dragons do not share magic. There could be greater effects than we know, borrowing or taking it from them. Until we know more, you cannot risk using your magic abilities to call on their power."

Crimson's shoulders slumped.

Ferruginous looked at Bowen, who now looked impatient, and said, "I have asked our scribe, Lazuli, to search the archives for information. Much of what we know about Jasper is from legends, and we must find facts. I will let you know when we have found more information. We must conclude and tend to other matters."

"I will send word to Hornblende and see what he thinks of this power—and what effect it has on dragon-kind," said Olivine. She turned her eyes toward Crimson.

The icy-cold stare of the dragon unnerved her. For the first time since she had become a keeper, there was a dragon she didn't trust. She was her father's dragon, but something about her made Crimson wary. Crimson dismissed the feeling. It was probably because she had shared her power, and nothing more.

"How do I know which magic I am using?" Crimson said. It all seemed to feel the same.

"When you are calling on Covelli's power to form gills, that is dragon magic," Amber said. "When you call on any other dragon's power, it is Magi magic. I know it may not seem like much of a distinction now, but you will learn how to tell the difference. We do not know enough yet about your powers. Just do not call the magic of other dragons, nor the magic from stones, until you have had Magi training and we have found out more. I will come tomorrow at dawn to begin your training."

Covelli and Crimson returned to the reeds with the promise that she would not call upon Magi magic. Crimson wished she could have seen her father more, but whatever news he had brought back from Alannador seemed to be very important. She was used to her father always disappearing on dragon-keeper or Elder business. She wished she could have had more time with him. Crimson found a dense patch of reeds and curled up with Covelli, letting the dragon magic flow between them, calming her mind.

CHAPTER 6

*L*AZULI, the scribe, looked over the hieroglyphs in the archive cave once again.

It was a jumbled mess, as if many scribes had written new information along with the old. Many of the old caves had been lost to erosion. Even in the depths of the mountain, water often found its way in and chipped away at the remains of history. Lazuli held the glow stone in her mouth, using its light to read and study. The hard stone pressed against her teeth, making her uncomfortable, but Ferruginous had tasked her with finding information: to find out why a young Norterridane named Crimson had the ability to copy dragon powers, and why the young dragon Azuran had shared his powers with the serpents. There was much to learn about how dragon power worked. These secrets were either unknown or forgotten long ago. Lazuli reread the archives about Jasper for days and only found limited clues about her time as a keeper. She had hoped that if she could find out more information on Jasper, it would lead her to answers about Crimson.

Jasper was able to use adult dragon powers, like Crimson had done, and Lazuli was determined to find out how this was possible. Why hadn't the previous scribes written more information about Jasper? It was almost as if they had erased her from history, but why?

Lazuli dropped the glow stone near the back wall and leaned in. She studied every etch, every mark, trying to find clues. She squinted in the dimly lit cave and looked past the black-and-gray fur of her snout at the symbols on the wall. A small crack in the stone, and near it an unfamiliar symbol. Where had that come from?

Lazuli placed a claw in the crack, and some small bits of stone fell away.

She moved her claw carefully along the crack. A larger piece broke off, and behind it was a symbol carved into the next layer of stone.

Someone had covered up the wall with stone. *Who would do such a thing? A Magi? why?*

Underneath the top layer of stone lay some strange and unfamiliar symbols.

It was common knowledge that Jasper had somehow saved the dragons from a plague. But there was no record of how she had stopped it from spreading to the soils of Genorrdia. One group of symbols was very clear, and they read, "beware the cave-dwellers."

A chill moved down Lazuli's spine to the tip of her tail, and she shook her fur to rid herself of the feeling. *It's in the past*, she told herself. *Perhaps I can use the known symbols to decipher the meanings of these unknown ones.*

Lazuli wanted to study further, but she had to let Ferruginous know about her findings and get his permission to remove the top layer of the archives. Lazuli ran up through the passages of the Underground. She passed several of the other archive caverns and came to the five-chambered cavern that made up the Elders' cave.

Ferruginous was always in a meeting. Lazuli perked up her ears as she hovered at the entrance to the Elders' cave. She walked in slowly, paw by paw.

"The serpents may still return if they are indeed wanting to link with the dragon hatchlings for power," a voice said.

"No, I think not. If they wanted the hatchlings, they would not have released the ones they had," another voice said. Lazuli recognized it as Beryl, chief of the guard.

"We should be worrying about the growing population of cave lizards," he said. "An increase in the gazelle population with the rains has caused an increase in our enemies. More have been seen lurking near the city."

"Perhaps the serpents forgot about the young dragons as they bolted, the cowards," another voice said. Lazuli did not recognize it.

"They are definitely not cowards. All would flee rather than face an enemy they cannot conquer. I would like to see you go against crystalline-enhanced fire," Beryl snarled.

Lazuli peeked around the corner and stepped inside.

Ferruginous raised a paw to quiet the room. "Prepare to fortify the lower tunnels and have more warriors patrol. Cave lizards are the immediate threat, and some have been seen near Crystal Lake. We will discuss ways to fortify the upper tunnels later, and keep the additional patrols in case the serpents do return."

Magic was scarce now, more so than it had been

in years, and fortifying the tunnels would mean using more magic that could be saved for healing. Norterridane had relied so much upon magic since the dragons had come to Genorrdia. Lazuli wondered how they would live without it.

Ferruginous walked up to his scribe. "What brings you here today?"

"I found something hidden in the southern cave, behind the archives."

"Hidden?" The old dog's eyes turned pensive.

"Yes, behind the stone."

"Show me."

Lazuli led the Elder down the tunnels to the cave where she had dropped the glow stone. The small crack in the wall seemed bigger now as she gazed at it again.

Ferruginous examined the wall and scraped lightly with his long claws.

"You were right to have called me. Transcribe the symbols to newer caverns, and uncover what is written."

"You don't know what it is?" Lazuli said.

"These are newer caverns, and for someone to hide this means it is very important. I want a report as soon as you are done."

"Of course," Lazuli said, bowing her head down as Ferruginous left the cave.

A FEW DAYS LATER, with the help of the Magi, most of the archives had been transferred by magic to other chambers in the Elders' cave, having to expand the archive caves out into the five-chambered den. Amber stood by the remaining hieroglyphs. Lazuli watched as she carved a symbol onto the magic stone. Amber touched the wall with one paw, her other placed on the stone. The symbols lifted off the wall and painted themselves on Amber's body before vanishing into the stone. Amber picked up the stone in her mouth and walked to the new caverns in the Elders' cave. She placed her paw back on the stone, and the symbols etched themselves onto the wall in the same pattern and position that they had been in on the lower caves.

"That is amazing," Lazuli said.

The next step was translation. That would take longer, so Lazuli started right away. Opal, a white-and-gray spotted Norterridane with rounded ears, scanned the archives with Lazuli.

"Some of these symbols are very confusing,"

Lazuli said as she focused on the wall. "Something about the cave-dwellers."

Opal moved closer to the wall, the glow stone in her mouth adding light to the symbols.

"A dragon wrote these symbols!" she said, dropping the stone to the floor.

"Dragons carved out these newer caves for the Elders, when dragon keeping first started, but I've never heard of them creating hieroglyphs," Opal said.

"But what do they mean?"

"It's going to be hard to decipher them on our own. Perhaps we can get a dragon to translate."

"We will have to transfer these symbols as well. Let's get Amber down here."

"We can have her transfer the symbols to the outer cliff wall for the dragons to read."

Lazuli looked over the symbols again. Why would a dragon write on this cave wall, and why would they cover the symbols? She shook her head. It just didn't make sense.

Lazuli stood just outside the Elders' cave on ledge of the massive cliff. Dragon messengers would come directly to this den entrance and speak with the

Elders. Forest dragons visited most often. Their ability to camouflage their scales to almost any terrain, making them invisible, made them the ideal messengers for Genorrdia. Olivine had been here earlier, but now black wings could be seen coming over the mountain from quite a distance away. Wingbeats brought with them the scent of dragons.

Jet, an Obsidian dragon, landed on the cliff. His black scales glittered in the sun, and the large spines on his back and neck were pointed and sharp. Hot air escaped his nostrils as he focused his black eyes on Lazuli.

Lazuli crouched instinctively, then mustered up the courage to whisper, "Greetings."

Jet moved his long neck, bringing his head close to her snout. She cleared her throat and said again, "Greetings." *Good, it came out louder.* His large black snakelike eye turned on her, and her legs shook.

"Stop pestering the young pup," Ferruginous's bold voice said through the Elders' cave opening. "Glad to see you, Jet. Any news of Azuran?"

Jet let out a heartful chuckle. "Nice to meet you. It was just too much to resist." His eyes seemed calm and caring now. "Such fear you Norterridane have of dragons."

"And with good reason," Ferruginous said.

"My searches have been fruitless. I shall search the forest again for Azuran, and the dark mountains after, but if he wants to stay hidden, it won't be hard. What is it that I can do for you? The pack that found me said it was urgent," Jet said to Lazuli.

"Well, we found some interesting symbols in our archive caves—the ones the dragons helped build—and they're dragon symbols. We were hoping you could translate them."

"Show me," Jet said, tapping his braided tail along the wall.

Lazuli walked along the wall outside of the Elders' cave. "Pardon me," she said as she came up to his tail. He moved it out of the way, and Lazuli showed him what the Magi had transcribed.

"Symbols are missing."

"We transferred all the ones we found."

"It says a keeper and a dragon stole a stone from the cave-dwellers, and that the whereabouts should never be revealed. But it also says something about a message—an important message. There is definitely something missing. Are there any other caves with messages?"

"The cave-dwellers cave?" Lazuli said. "There is a cave near the ocean that Crimson found that belonged to them. She said there were many symbols there."

"The missing symbols could be there," Jet said. "I could take you."

"No," Ferruginous said. "I will send a pack. You can continue your search for Azuran. I think that is a more pressing matter."

"Why would a dragon hide such a simple message?" Lazuli said.

"Dragons do not hide simple messages. There is something they wanted to keep hidden, and probably for good reason," Jet said, "if only to keep the cave-dwellers from finding out information about this stone they stole. If there is nothing further, I will continue my mission."

Ferruginous nodded. Jet dove off the cliff and flew away over the Black Mountains.

"But if they wanted to keep secrets from the cave dwellers, why would they put messages in the abandoned caves?" Lazuli said.

"You will have to find those answers, " Ferruginous said, "The dwellers have been gone from Genorrdia for hundreds of years."

Lazuli looked off over the cliff edge toward the redwood forest. Nothing about this felt right.

MALACHITE and Andalus crawled along the hill, staying as low as they could in the grasses.

What magic was Fairburn talking about in this lake? If it was a magic stone, Malachite would find it.

The serpents moved over the ridge and peered down toward the lake as the last light faded. There, a few hills away, moving amongst the reeds beyond the hill, was a small red Norterridane.

Malachite grinned. Was this the magic Fairburn was detecting? He had heard of the magic power this Norterridane held. He had not seen the wall of fire she had created, but Sodal had died because of it.

Andalus moved forward, and Malachite grabbed one of his arms.

"What are you doing?" Andalus said.

"We cannot go down there."

"There are no dragons around."

"That is the one. The Norterridane that called upon the white flames," Malachite said. "I am not stupid enough to go against her."

"So how do we investigate the lake?"

"We don't; not yet," Malachite said. "We need to find out more about these Norterridane. We didn't know enough when first we attacked, and we don't know enough now."

"How are we going to do that? We can't get close enough to the city."

"But there is someone who can. Azuran."

"Azuran? You trust him?"

"Onixian raised him, and he fought with us in battle."

"You cannot be serious," Andalus said. "He is a dragon."

"A dragon who desperately wants to be a serpent," Malachite said, "and we are going to give him the opportunity to earn it."

"We haven't seen him since the battle. How can you be sure he is here?"

"I saw him."

"And you didn't tell Onixian?"

"I choose what information Schorl should know."

MALACHITE FLEW low over the desert wasteland, dragon power flowing through his body. He felt almost invincible, and he just might be. The power from the Obsidian he had killed was more than he had ever gained from magic stones alone. For now, it fulfilled him. He knew this would not last, just as the other kills did not last. He always craved more magic.

Malachite and Andalus caught up with the serpents in a desert wasteland on the eastern part of Genorrdia. Dry, cracked soil flaked off the ground as Malachite's feet crunched upon it. The group moved on, walking for hours while brushing away their footprints upon the ground, often flying over the desert to rest their feet. The wasteland seemed to go on forever.

"I have seen the red Norterridane," Malachite said, walking next to Fairburn. "Is that the magic you sensed?"

"No, not at all. My magic does not sense magical creatures, or we could find and kill dragons easily. But since we know what power that magical dog has, perhaps we can keep an eye on it."

"My thoughts exactly. What do you think of using Azuran for the task?"

"Risky."

"So you are unsure of him as well."

"He is Obsidian."

"Onixian trusts him."

"Yes, he does."

"Then Onixian will be the one to persuade him," Malachite said, hovering his tail above the hot, dry earth, "but he must also be prepared to kill him."

"Better to have an Obsidian on our side. If he can be persuaded, it would be a great advantage."

WHEN THE SUN once again peaked over the mountains, Malachite called the serpents to rest. Now, with his body still, he felt a craving for more magic, like a flutter in his stomach—faint, yes, but it was there. It was always there, threatening to creep up and consume him.

The magic stones could ward off the hunger for months, even years, but it always returned. In time, only the hunger would matter. His mind had to remain focused, or the Schorl would perish.

Malachite lay upon the cracked earth. The sunrays

warmed his scales. He closed his eyes, letting a feeling of peace roll over his body.

"Malachite, I have found something," Fairburn said.

Malachite rolled to his feet. "What is it?"

"Some magic stones, not far from here, and close to the surface." Fairburn led Malachite away from the serpents to a patch of scaly, cracked earth. They dug into the earth. The cool underlayers were welcome as the sunrays grew stronger. Malachite grabbed handfuls of sand with four of his arms and threw it behind him. He could sense the magic now on his own. He braced himself and lowered one arm down into the hole. He felt the stone and pulled up a small yellow smoky quartz. The power pulsated in his hand.

"Hesson," Malachite called, and the serpent guard approached. "For your loyalty," Malachite said, handing Hesson the stone. Hesson nodded and swallowed down the stone. His body shuddered for a moment, and his scales shifted slightly to a darker gray.

"We must leave now before the sunrays are too strong in this desert," Fairburn said. "We can come back for more stones later."

"We'll fly east and far past the volcanic mountain Xenoti," Malachite said to the resting serpents. "We'll move along the shoreline until we reach our destination. Keep a lookout for dragons, and alert us if any are seen. We cannot afford a battle right now. The stone-reader says the mountain will be a haven. We follow her."

Of the hundred serpents that had come with Malachite for what seemed an easy victory, only fifty remained. Many had died, mostly from Obsidian flames as they'd retreated, and others had fled back to Calimdural. Malachite must prove he could lead, or another serpent would challenge him and take his place, or try to kill him as he slept. None here would dare, but among those back in Calimdural, he had many enemies. He had to convince them that he alone was the rightful ruler and, by his own decree, the only one who could save the Schorl.

The serpents flew low along the mountain range for hours, each looking out for signs of magic stones or dragons. The barren mountains did not provide cover. The treeless mountains to the west and the ocean to the east. Sea dragons were always a threat as the ocean was near. But not here on Genorrdia.

Malachite's scales soaked up the sun, heating his body to the core.

He looked down once again at the ocean. It could provide a peaceful break for his wings.

He turned in mid-flight, rotating his bat-like wings in a circular motion to stay in the air. He signaled for the scouts to scan the ocean waters. His scouts, Andalus and Hesson, were the most trusted king's guard. Malachite shared the power he found with them and they stayed loyal.

Andalus and Hesson closed their wings and dove for the ocean. Their decent was so swift that one might have thought they would crash, but they opened their wings to stop at the precise moment and landed gracefully on the breach, bracing the impact with their enormous hind legs. Then they disappeared into the water.

Malachite roared, signaling the rest of the Schorl serpents to land on a semi-steep slope to rest.

They covered their bodies with their enormous gray wings, which blended in slightly with the landscape. At least from far away, they would look like large gray stones. All but Onixian.

Malachite found Onixian toward the front of the serpent clan. He was not hard to spot, being the only serpent with shiny black scales. Onixian had gone to kill an Obsidian hatchling, inadvertently becoming attached to the dragon. But in sparing his life, Onixian shared the Obsidian's power, and his gray serpent scales had turned black. Onixian was once one of

Malachite's lead scouts. He had become so strong so young, but Malachite couldn't trust him now that he had shared power with a dragon instead of killing it. Azuran had been useful, but dragons were the enemy.

Malachite walked over to the young and powerful serpent. Malachite had often thought of killing Azuran, but he didn't have the power to go against both Onixian and Azuran, at least not yet. And now he needed the dragon.

"Fairburn says there is a great power by the lake. I want to find it."

"And you need me to go with her to find it?" Onixian said. "I found Genorrdia for you, and look where we are."

Malachite held back his anger. "I have found Azuran."

"He's alive?"

"Yes."

"Why do you care?" Onixian sneered.

"I want you to talk to him about going on a mission," Malachite said.

Onixian eyed Malachite suspiciously.

"We need Azuran to convince the Norterridane to tell him what the power in the lake is and how to get it." Malachite leaned in closer to Onixian. The sun's heat beat down on his scales, and he shifted his wings over his head. "Tell him that we want to find a way to become more powerful, and either the Norterridane knows of this power under the lake, or she knows where they keep the dragon eggs. Azuran can find out about both."

"Why would Azuran agree?"

"Because I am willing to let him be one of us. Not just live among us, but earn a place with the Schorl."

Onixian turned his head, studying Malachite as if trying to see past his words. Malachite expected him to be cautious.

He hoped Onixian would agree; otherwise, he would have to find a way to convince Azuran to join him. He couldn't have an uncontrollable dragon living among Schorl.

Legend had it that Obsidian dragons came from the volcanoes. Schorl most likely came from the icy depths of Calimdural. He refused to believe that Schorl and dragons were once the same species. Lies dragons told to make Schorl feel inferior, as if they were a lessor creation made from dragons themselves.

Wingbeats and splashing water turned his head.

Hesson trudged onto the beach and flew to the mountainside.

"The ocean is clear and there is much life inside. The waters are warm; nothing like Calimdural."

Andalus landed by Hesson, water dripping off his scales. "We should travel the rest of the way under the ocean."

"Brilliant," Malachite said, nodding to Onixian and leaving him with his thoughts. "Let us move to the ocean."

The serpents readily agreed.

Malachite plunged into the water, cooling his scales. The icy waters of Calimdural chilled the bones, and they only hunted in the ocean if there were seafins about, but these waters were refreshing.

Malachite swam past a sandy drop-off until he was completely covered under the ocean waves.

Schorl could hold their breath for hours under the right conditions. The water wrapped around Malachite's scales, filling him with content. Many ocean creatures swam near, and reminded him of his life on Calimdural. He detested the taste of ocean animals, but when hungry, they would do. He let his body float in the water as if he were a lifeless rock. He waited until one of the larger fish swam near his chest. His six arms moved in unison, trapping it in a flurry of claws. He floated to the surface to enjoy his meal.

He ate his fill and called the serpents to follow him underneath the currents. They moved almost in unison under the waves. The ocean waters cooled, and the sun shone less and less upon the ocean. Tall, dark mountains loomed in the distance. Like giant pillars of black stone, they created a wall of shadows, so tall they seemed to touch the sky. Icy white-tipped peaks spiraled up thousands of feet and vanished in the clouds, like sharp claws raising out of the earth to capture their prey. Malachite had never seen such mountains, not even on Calimdural. A shiver went down his spine, but not from the cold.

Fairburn approached, holding the magic stone glowing in her claws. "There are magic stones here. Perhaps we will not need to get whatever magic is in the lake."

"Or we can have both," Malachite said.

"The magic seems so deep in the lake; I fear that only magic will be able to retrieve it. This wasn't here before, when Onixian and I searched Genorrdia. Something must have awakened a dormant power."

"Something with the power to awaken sleeping magic," Malachite said, thinking again of the red Norterridane and the power she had created.

"Let's search this mountain. If we find Azuran, we can deal with the lake," Andalus said.

The serpents hiked up the mountainside. Their sharp claws dug into snow and ice. Malachite clenched his claws, shivered uncontrollably again, and stared at the mountainous pillars of ice. Even as it chilled him, the hunger for magic burned inside.

Malachite turned to see Onixian at his side.

"I will talk to Azuran," Onixian said.

"I saw him near Crystal Lake. He was headed toward a valley near Mount Xenoti. Find him and bring him here."

Onixian nodded and flew away.

A broad smile spread across Malachite's face.

CHAPTER 8

AZURAN clawed again at the rocky slope, knocking off large chunks onto the ground. The cave was nearly finished. He looked down from the small, rocky mountainside. The valley was lush and green with trees, bushes, and grasses. Shade covered the grasses as the sun began to set. Deer grazed far below, oblivious to his presence, filling his heart with joy. Mountain goats grazed upon the slopes and rocky portions of the valley. Azuran swung his tail, pushing the stones away from the entrance, and walked inside. He turned around several times, measuring the size of the cave. Just a bit more, and it would be perfect.

Azuran scratched his lower jaw. It had been itching lately, and he was certain it was something in the stone caves that made it so. Nothing else bothered him. His blue eyes looked around the cave at the dust he had created by carving the stone. An image of Crimson flashed in his mind. In a similar cave and with a feeling—joy perhaps. Then it was gone. He wondered what life would be like if he took her advice and flew to Alannador. He was alone out here. A sudden, sharp pain registered in his right forefoot. The wound that Malachite had inflicted had long since healed. A circular scar was all that remained. Why did it hurt now? He grunted and moved from the cave for some fresh air.

Wind blew past his nostrils. Azuran flicked his tongue, tasting the scents on the air; grass, deer and deer droppings, flowers, and several small mice. There, among the many flavors of the valley, a serpent. Approaching from the north. Azuran peered out of the cave and recognized the glassy black serpent. He flew to meet him.

"I thought you were dead," he said, slamming the serpent playfully with his tail.

"Likewise," Onixian said.

"Where are the others?"

"On those icy mountains to the north. Malachite told me where to find you."

Azuran landed on the grass. "What does he want?"

"Help in finding some great hidden power."

"I thought when the dragons came, you all would leave Genorrdia."

"You underestimate the Schorl's craving for power. Why are you still here?

"This is my home," Azuran said.

"I'm hungry; let's hunt," Onixian called as he leapt off the slope and into the air.

Azuran opened his wings and jumped into the air after Onixian. With the wind in his face, his heart pounded with anticipation, and thoughts of finding and killing his dinner was all that remained.

The deer and mountain goats bolted from the valley toward the forest.

"Let's go for the goats," Onixian said. "Their horns can damage Schorl scales. They put up a good fight, but we always win." He began to descend.

The setting sun changed the valley. Azuran could see almost as well at night as in the day. The land changed colors, but the sharpness and clarity stayed the same. Azuran tasted the air again. The goats were not far ahead, their scent thick in the air.

Onixian scanned the area. "Circle to the left," he instructed, moving right to cut off a large white-furred goat. Onixian landed between the goat and its herd. The other goats ran up the mountain to the south and into a dense evergreen forest. The white goat turned and ran up higher on the slope.

"Why run?" Onixian said. "You know we'll catch you anyway."

Azuran laughed and landed.

Onixian's muscled legs moved him effortlessly across the rocky landscape, claws grating the ground with each step. The goat was large, half a serpent height at least. Its large curved horns looked as if they could cause a painful blow against most creatures, possibly breaking bone. Its hooves pounded against the ground, and its curved horns dipped low. Its eyes watched the predators closely.

Azuran leapt into the air, drawing the goat's attention. It stood strong and defiant, and charged the dragon.

Azuran growled and let it hit him. The force was stronger than he anticipated, and he fell to the ground. His four legs were nowhere near as strong as Onixian's two.

Onixian laughed behind him. "The Obsidian is defeated by a goat ... Get up and kill it."

The goat was half Azuran's size, thick with bulky muscles used for ascending steep, rocky ledges.

Azuran picked himself off the ground, pressing his wings firmly against his body. He ran, full stride, toward the goat on all fours. He opened his wings at the last moment to aid his leap off the ground— nowhere as high as a Schorl could jump, but high enough to land on the goat's back. Horns slammed into his face as the goat kicked and fought. The pressure annoyed him, but the horns didn't hurt. The goat slammed him again. He shook his head.

I am supposed to be invincible.

Azuran flapped his wings. Adrenaline rushed through his body. He clawed at the goat's fur, making deep gashes in its side. Then he bit down hard on its neck, and the goat's horns slammed into the side of his face. The goat was much stronger than he had thought it would be. He tried lifting the enormous goat into the air. He pulled up with his front and back legs, but only managed to get it a few feet off the ground. *Hopefully, I will be stronger when I am older. This is embarrassing.*

Onixian walked to his side, smirking. Serpents were always smirking.

"Oh, you think this is funny?" Azuran cried, his arms struggling to keep the horns at bay.

"Yes, I do," he chuckled. "Let it go."

Azuran lessened his grip on the goat. Onixian

lifted the goat effortlessly with his two top arms and threw it into the nearest boulder with such force it wobbled as it got to its hooves. Onixian moved forward and stabbed his tusks through the goat's heart. Azuran shook his head again, watching his mentor. It was Onixian's favorite way to kill.

Onixian made it look so easy. Azuran sighed. "I would have killed it."

"Eventually," Onixian said. "But I am hungry."

"Let's eat our fill and take the rest back to the mountain; I need some bones for my cave. If you want, I'll kill another for you."

A short time later, Onixian brought Azuran a small goat.

"Really, you couldn't have brought a bigger one?"

"Learn to kill the big ones yourself." Onixian chuckled again.

Azuran snorted and opened his mouth; blue flames charred the carcass. Onixian jumped back from the heat.

Azuran clawed away at the burnt fur and sank his teeth into the goat. The flavor tingled on his tongue.

"I wonder what it's like to breathe fire so hot that I could turn this goat to ashes."

"I wonder what it's like to breath fire," Onixian said.

"I'm serious. If Malachite had given me the sardonyx, we might have had a chance at winning."

"I doubt you would have turned your kind to ashes. You didn't fight one dragon."

Azuran took another bite of the goat.

"Have you thought about Malachite's offer?" Onixian said.

"I don't trust him."

"Neither do I, but just because we work with him doesn't mean we have to give him the mysterious power."

Azuran swallowed another bite of goat meat. "Take it for ourselves?"

"You and I would be even more powerful. Nothing could kill us; we would be the most powerful creatures that ever lived."

Azuran let the words sink in. If he had that power, he wouldn't fear retribution from his own kind. The Obsidians would fear him. He did not know the dragon side of the war, but the serpents said that dragons kill serpents without warning, even the young. Onixian did not want to lead the serpents; he was just afraid to die. Could he, Azuran, lead both dragons and serpents?

Azuran chewed a few more mouthfuls, wiping the

blood from his face. His jaw itched again; perhaps it was the goat blood.

He moved his clawed hand up to his cheek. It itched like when he had shed his gray hatchling scales. The goat blood and bits of fur must be irritating his scales. A sting registered in his hand, and blood dripped from a small opening. Something had cut his impenetrable skin. He moved up his claw again. A small bone, sharp like a dragon tooth, protruded from his lower jaw. He pulled his other forefoot up to feel the left side of his cheek. A bump had formed there as well, though nothing sharp had yet emerged from it.

"Do dragons grow tusks?" he asked Onixian, because tusks seemed to be growing out of his skin.

Onixian stopped eating and looked up. Bits of the mountain goat dripped down his face. He moved closer to inspect the small gray bones that had begun growing from Azuran's lower jaw.

"What …?" he said, eyes focusing as he moved in closer to inspect. "It appears that you are. Serpents grow tusks within the first few months of their birth. But dragons never grow any. We'll ask Fairburn what it means."

"Why Fairburn? You all seem to rely on her word a lot."

"She is a stone-reader. Their magic is more powerful than all others, and they are wise. They help lead the king and Schorl to greatness. Without her, we would never have found Genorrdia."

Azuran took a large bite of goat meat and swallowed it down. Onixian picked up his dead goat and spread his wings.

Azuran lifted what was left of his small goat and followed Onixian. He said nothing on the flight to the mountain. He watched the landscape change from vibrant to barren and desolate. Pillars of ice jutted out of snowcapped mountains, and cold wind blew against Azuran's scales. But the landscape could not quell his pride. He was growing tusks, and he had been chosen to find what may be the most powerful magic any had seen. He thought of what Onixian had said about keeping the power. He had shared enough of his power with Onixian. He would get this power, and he would take it all.

CHAPTER 9

ONIXIAN threw his goat carcass into his cave. "Wait here. I will get Fairburn."

Azuran nodded, dropping his goat to the ground. He continued his meal, looking up occasionally at the caves the serpents had built in this icy wasteland. They were made where the soil was frozen, but not where there was solid rock. The serpents looked at him cautiously. Azuran ignored their stares. While he had to be cautious of Malachite's and Andalus's red-tipped tusks and claws, no other serpents were a threat.

A flutter of wings reached his ears. He unconsciously tasted the air. Fairburn and Onixian had come.

Fairburn stared at Azuran for a moment; her red eyes looked gray in the dark as she studied his face. She touched his scaled maw and the hard, bony tusk in his skin. Azuran admired her. She never seemed intimidated by the other serpents, or by him. She didn't seem to fear him at all. She was intelligent, and levelheaded. She did not let the hunger, as the serpents called it, sway her judgment. Perhaps it was because she was a stone-reader.

Fairburn lifted the magic-detecting stone and let it glow by his face. The sudden light temporarily blinded him; he closed his eyes tightly.

"Is he turning into a serpent?" Onixian asked.

Azuran did not expect a definite answer. For how would Fairburn know? He opened his eyes, letting them adjust to the pale light. This was the first time a serpent had ever bonded with a dragon, and the first time a dragon lived among serpents.

"It would appear so," said Fairburn. "It could be the bond you share." She studied him a moment longer. Her lip curled, and scaled nose wrinkled.

Something about the way she did it made Azuran wonder if she was pretending to be disgusted by him.

"It's not just tusks. Have you ever heard of a dragon that tasted the air as we do?"

"No," Onixian said. "I hadn't thought of it before now."

"How well is your sense of smell?" Fairburn asked Azuran.

"I could tell it was you who was coming, and I knew Onixian was on his way to find me long before I saw him."

"You are benefiting from your link with Onixian, for Obsidian dragons do not have the best sense of smell, which is one reason we have evaded the dragon scout so long. It makes sense; you shared your scales and power. Perhaps you will share Onixian's strengths as well."

"He will be a strange dragon indeed if he starts sprouting extra arms." Onixian laughed.

"It would be good if he did. The ugliness of dragons annoys me," Fairburn said flatly, ignoring his jest.

Azuran took it with a grain of salt. He heard such comments often. He and Onixian had lived alone for as long as he could remember. Onixian had been like a father to him. But when he matured, and his scales had turned glassy black, he and Onixian had gone to live with the serpents and fought in the Norterridane battle.

"Perhaps Malachite will hate him less if he looks

more like a serpent," Onixian reasoned.

"He hates you both. Perhaps we need to find and bond with more dragons. We never had the chance to see if we could bond with dragons that are not Obsidian. We released the hatchlings too soon."

"So if we cannot find this mystical lake power, we can have a backup plan of getting hatchlings."

"Or dragon eggs," Fairburn said. "I will let Malachite know about these new findings."

Azuran wondered if there was a way to break the bond, but he did not know enough about dragon powers to find out. Perhaps Crimson would know. He must learn more from her.

When Fairburn left, Onixian said to Azuran, "The Norterridane must know where the dragons lay their eggs." His eyes brightened with delight. "And you will find them and bring them back."

"Fine plan, but why would they trust me?" Azuran said.

"You are a dragon, and the red Norterridane knew you. You just have to find her, convince her that you are on their side, and convince her that we have left Genorrdia. I am sure it won't take much."

Azuran nodded, staying silent to the fact that he had already seen her. The serpents wanted dragon eggs? Well, perhaps Azuran could use their power instead, like Onixian had done with his. But he needed more information. A shudder moved through Azuran's body. Dragons also didn't crave magic. It must be this link that was making him power hungry. He didn't mind it though; power made him feel alive.

Azuran took the goat carcass up to a solitary, ice-covered peak. The small cut on his hand stung, reminding him of his battle with the goat. He couldn't tell Onixian. No, he could not let him see weakness. He rubbed the spikes above his ear; a strange sound had begun. It took him a minute to realize it was a song. A song he had heard before. The song Crimson had reminded him of.

Glimpses of running through red-colored willows flowed in and out of his mind. The melody continued, and there in his mind was Crimson, walking with him in the willows. Another young dragon with green eyes was beside him. He could almost hear its voice.

Chalcedony?

He remembered. His sister running though the red willows, following him on another adventure. Truth be told, he had remembered much after the waterfall, but in order to survive, he had hidden how much had come back to him. He rubbed his talons along the scar on this right hand, the sting taking him from his memory.

SNOW GLITTERED DOWN upon the spiraled mountain, adding more to the already packed layer on the peak. His sharp Obsidian claws cut easily through the deep stone. Serpents, whose claws were much weaker, carved their homes in the lower areas of the mountain, where dirt mixed with eroded stone. It had taken quite a bit of work to dig past a foot of ice to the rock itself, and then to carve out a cave big enough to fit his growing body. Onixian had spoken often about the cold continent of Calimdural. It was cold in these parts of the mountains, and barren. Though Azuran had never been to Calimdural, he could imagine the resemblance. He preferred the warm summers of the aspen forest that had been his home, only because of the abundance of deer to be found.

Azuran clawed at the rock, chipping it off piece by piece with his invincible black talons. He paused briefly to stretch his front leg and continued his work. The cold clawed at his scales, and even though his body radiated heat from within, he wondered if the mountain had the ability to end that heat forever. Serpents were used to the cold. Something in their makeup had made the cold tolerable. Perhaps it was magic, perhaps an inherited ability. Perhaps they were just willing to die.

He guffawed at the thought. The Schorl were a strong race, and he had learned how to be strong from them.

THE BLACK MOUNTAIN peaks jutted up in the distance, icy and cold, promising death to any who ventured to the high northern reaches and could not fly away. Azuran gave whispered thanks into the wind that he had been born with wings. He was not sure whom he was thanking, but whatever magic had brought him into the world, surely something had created it. He sometimes imagined the wind could hear him, and one time, he had wished for rain on a particularly hot day, and it had rained a few hours later. He hadn't told Onixian though. He wouldn't have believed him anyway.

Azuran scanned the snowy mountains. No sign of life, not for miles. He groaned. Why would they want to stay here? The valley was much more comfortable.

He flew down to Onixian's cave.

"Why are we here?" he said, swishing his tail in the snow.

"Obsidian dragons are searching the forest for us," Onixian shrugged. "They will probably kill you too for fighting with us."

Azuran glared at him. Was there a chance the dragons would understand him? Would they take him in even though he had been raised as serpent? Is that what he wanted? Onixian had told him dragons were evil. They killed thousands of serpents, sparing none, even the young. They had never been given the chance to see if they could overcome the magic hunger.

"You're probably right."

"I am right," Onixian said.

Still, when the dragons had come to save the Norterridane, something had stirred inside. And when he'd met the dragon Covelli and spoke with her in dragon tongue, the feeling had come again. A feeling he had never known before: longing.

Malachite flew overhead, surveying the land. Azuran flinched at the sight. He flew back up to his cave in the ice. He was used to being alone, but every so often, he felt the need for a different kind of companionship. Sometimes he would dream of the green eyes of his sister looking at him and felt connected. But as always, when he awoke, it was gone. He spoke again to the wind. "Will this great power fill this emptiness I feel? Is it power I crave, like the serpent I am becoming?"

There was no answer. Just the cold chill of the night.

CHAPTER 10

CRIMSON looked down at the stone. It glowed a pale yellow. Amber slid her claw across it, scratching two lines. Her claw glowed as she called on the stone's magic.

"It's similar to using dragon power. You can hold it until ready to use, but you can only store so much power."

"Is that why I collapsed on the battlefield?" Crimson asked.

"You were channeling too much power; normally, only Magi with years of practice can use that much." Amber turned toward the hillside, where Crimson had attempted to make a den. Magic moved from Amber's claws, out toward the mud-filled hole. The mud hardened, forming a tunnel and den.

"I can see that magic moving!"

"A useful ability of Magi," Amber said. "You can also feel it moving, like you said you feel the dragon magic."

"Can we do anything with magic? Anything at all?"

"No, not exactly. We can only manipulate elements and nature. For example, I used water to build the den. First hollowing out the tunnel, and then extracting the water so it would harden. Then I used pressure to harden the soil."

"It doesn't really seem similar to dragon magic."

"It is similar, but not the same, because it is a different type of magic."

Crimson looked at the stone; it was glowing less now that the magic had been used.

"Try it," Amber said.

Crimson placed her claw on the stone.

"Feel the magic, like when you call upon the fire."

Crimson concentrated. Blue fire sprang from her claws.

"That is not quite it. You just used your innate magic. You need to draw on the stone, like you do with dragons."

Crimson scraped the stone, concentrating on the magic within it.

"I don't feel it."

"It should be automatic," Amber said, then placed a claw on the stone next to Crimson. Amber moved the magic from the stone into her paw, then placed it on Crimson. The magic flowed into her paw, onto her claws like a rainbow of colors: blues, greens, and golds. She turned over her paw. There was a tingle, like wind rustling her fur, but it was barely there.

"I feel it. But it is so subtle. Is that because the magic is almost gone?"

Amber looked at Crimson, her eyes saddened. "No, I do not think that is why. I think you are used to channeling much larger sources of magic. The feeling of drawing magic from stone is like nothing else in the world for a Magi who has never felt it; powerful and effortless."

Crimson turned her paw over once again, feeling the magic. Amber placed her paw on Crimson's and moved the magic back to the stone. "You will have to learn to pull the magic from the stone and place it back. Once you can do that, the real training—"

Amber sniffed the air and perked her ears. Crimson smelled it too: the scent of dragons and serpents.

A dark speck in the sky flew over the hills to the west, then flew down and vanished behind the hills.

"It is Azuran," Crimson said. Covelli pounced over, squeaking and hopping up and down.

"Seems suspicious if you ask me," Amber said, eyeing the hills. She sniffed again. "The Elders have been looking for him, and suddenly he is coming to find you?"

AZURAN CAME OVER THE HILLTOP, sending a rush of air through the reeds. Small gray bones protruded from his jaw. They were little, but there was no mistaking the resemblance to the serpents.

Crimson's fur raised almost unconsciously. She wanted to run but knew she had to stay and talk with him. Amber growled.

"Stay calm. He won't hurt us," Crimson said with as much conviction as she could. "Azuran, you're back."

Azuran moved his snout close to Covelli. Excitement danced in the dragon's eyes.

"Covelli," Crimson called, and the dragon moved by her side. Was it safe for her to be so close to him?

Amber stood back. "Crimson, he should see the Elders."

"Elders?" Azuran said.

"They protect us," Crimson said. "What do you want, Azuran?"

Azuran focused his blue eyes on her, as if he was trying to see into her mind. "I have heard of a great magical power in this lake. Do you know of it?"

"No," Crimson said.

Amber stood silent at Crimson's side.

"Maybe your Elders would know," Azuran said.

"We can go to the city and talk to the Elders. They may know."

"No. I'd rather go look now. It will be fun," Azuran said, his voice light and playful. "And you could ask them about it later."

"Now? And how do you propose we do that?" Crimson said. Azuran was searching for magic, and he smelled of serpents. She did not trust him.

"Covelli told me you share her power to breathe underwater; we can go now."

Crimson shot Covelli a questioning stare. The dragon moved between her legs and rubbed against her.

"How do you know about a power in Crystal Lake?" Crimson said.

Azuran stretched his wings, and warm air blew into Crimson's face.

"The serpents told him," Amber said.

Azuran stepped forward, his huge talons pressing into the mud. "Yes, the serpents told me. But I am curious about it." His forefoot was larger than Crimson's whole body. The scales lining his underside were smooth, and his tail moved like a snake as he moved past Crimson through the reeds toward the lake. "Come on, it will be an adventure, and you love to explore."

He was right, and he was using her love of adventure against her.

Crimson looked to Amber. "Go. I'll stay and wait for you. If you are not back soon—" *I'll alert the Elders*, her stern expression and tail wag said silently.

Crimson pushed past the plants growing at the lake's edge and waded into the open water. The cool water chilled her muzzle and the tips of her button ears. Covelli caught up to her with a few short strokes.

Crimson reached for the dragon power. The cool, breezy feeling of Covelli's dragon magic flowed through her mind and body. Gills formed, and she propelled herself through the water. The apprehension she felt going with Azuran down into the lake faded slightly as she swam. Fish darted out of the way. Crimson paddled after Azuran.

"Wait up," Crimson barked. Covelli slowed,

moving her head toward fish that swam by, smelling them with her enlarged nasal cavities. She lurched forward, catching one in her jaws. The dragon squealed in delight. Her purple eyes glowed with pride.

"Nice job!" Crimson said. Azuran swam by and shook his head. He pointed down at the large crevasse on the bottom of the lake. *A mysterious power in the lake that the serpents know about but not Norterridane, how is this possible?*

The water grew colder, and it was harder to breathe this deep in the lake. Azuran turned and swam to the surface. Light dimmed near the bottom of the lake. Crimson's eyes adjusted to the darkness, but it was harder to see underwater in the dark than on land. Her head began to ache, and Crimson wondered if the lack of oxygen was affecting Covelli as well. The dragon showed no signs of distress. She was circling and gliding around with seemingly endless energy.

Crimson gazed into the crevasse. There was no way to tell how deep the it was, nor any magic glow stones to guide the way. Crimson called on the dragon fire. Her claws lit up with a blue glow. The water boiled as it hit the magical fire. Fish darted away from the sudden light. The crevasse was made completely of slate, a hard gray metamorphic rock. Layer upon layer of slate disappearing into the darkness. As Crimson stared past the light of her claws, a cold ripple came over her. It was like dragon magic, but stronger and unpleasant behind the wall of stone. She shivered. Whatever it was, it didn't seem welcoming. Was this the magic Azuran was looking for?

Covelli looked down into the darkness and backed away, shaking her head.

Crimson let the flames from her claws vanish and swam over to her companion's side. "What do you think is down there?"

Covelli backed farther away.

"It does seem a bit scary. Azuran will not be able to come down here and take it. We will let the Elders know about this."

Crimson was unsettled by how it scared Covelli. Whatever magic was down there, even she could sense the darkness of it.

"Let's go home," she said, and Covelli readily agreed.

Swimming back toward the shore, Crimson caught a fish. Her barbed claws held it in place as she climbed onto the shore. Azuran was there waiting. "What did you find?"

"Nothing; it was too dark to see, and too deep."

"Too deep for a sea dragon?"

"Covelli didn't want to go."

Azuran turned to Covelli. Covelli squeaked and smashed back into the lake.

"What did you say to her?"

"That is not your concern," Azuran said, pressing his claws into the mud.

"Leave her alone."

"She could go and find the magic easily."

"Whatever it is, it's behind stone. It doesn't feel like good magic. You don't know what it is or what it will do."

Azuran growled and smoke came from his nostrils. "So you did find something?"

Amber stepped between them, fur raised. "Did you think it would be that easy: just tell the dragon to go get some powerful magic? If you are wanting the power for the serpents, then leave. You will find no help here."

Azuran snarled. Crimson jumped in front of Amber and called for his dragon magic, pulling on the waves of heat. Azuran swayed and backed away, his feet crushing reeds underneath. A wall of white fire sprang up between them.

"You can't just kill whoever you want," Crimson barked, holding on to his power. She could feel him weakening.

Azuran bared his teeth and roared.

Amber growled. "It's time for the dragon to go."

Azuran struggled to stand, clawing into the ground. He tapped his tail on the ground, sliding it back and forth.

"I shouldn't have done that, but she was …"

"I can't help you if I can't trust you," Crimson said, letting go of his power. She placed her paw on his scales for just a moment. "We could still go talk to the Elders."

Azuran shook his head.

"Come back as a friend, or not at all," Crimson said, keeping her eye on him as he stood and spread his wings. He turned and flew away over the hills.

"Crimson, we have to tell the Elders," Amber said.

Crimson had felt Azuran's power drain. The elders were right. Her power was dangerous.

CRIMSON and Covelli swam up the passageway to the Underground. There were several empty dens to the left and right. She shook her fur and turned to Covelli. "Stay here in this den. I have to find Beryl. If anything comes, go back into the lake."

The dragon nodded. Crimson knew this was risky, but she had to talk with Beryl. He would know what to do.

Crimson ran up one of the tunnels. These tunnels were rarely used. In recent years, cave lizards had become more of a threat and several times had come through the tunnel walls. Claw markings along the wall were reminders of when they had come. Crimson shrugged at that thought; her fire powers would be enough against the lizards. Only two things in this world frightened her, and one was that serpent Onixian. Perhaps years ago Norterridane used these tunnels more. But the water level changed so frequently that the dens were unusable.

What a waste, Crimson thought, and moved out into the tunnels, not too far away, and waited for a warrior to patrol.

"Crimson, what are you doing here?" a familiar voice said.

"Torbern," Crimson said, wagging her tail in friendship. What luck the warrior patrolling was her friend. They weren't close, but they had battled together, and that meant a lot among warriors. The scar across his tan face had been caused by none other than Azuran himself. She wondered how much she should tell him, or how he would feel about it. After all, he had never cared for a dragon.

"Did you bring your dragon here? I can smell it."

"Yes. Sorry, it could not be avoided. I need to speak with Beryl."

Torbern sniffed the air, fixated on the smell.

"Young dragons have a stronger smell," Crimson explained. "Most of the time, we cover it with Jasperillian or mud, but she is a sea dragon, so both are kind of pointless."

"Can I see it?"

"*Her* name is Covelli. I named her after covellite."

"That bluish-purple mineral?"

"Yeah. You can see her quickly, and then I need Beryl."

"Just a quick peek."

Crimson took Torbern to the small den opening. Covelli was curled up in a ball, her scaly head leaning on tiny webbed dragon paws.

"She is beautiful," he said, considering the dragon. "Much smaller than I thought. I don't know why I thought she would be large like the dragons that came to the battle." He placed a paw gently on her scales. "Wow, so soft."

Covelli opened her eyes for a second, closed them, and curled her tail and placed the fin over her head.

"Their scales harden when they mature. Did you see any when they moved the hatchlings to the caves before?"

"No. I was preparing for war and focused on battle, plus I think the Elders moved them in from other tunnels, not near the warrior dens. Will she wake up soon?"

"Maybe. Baby dragons sleep a lot. Can you please

get Beryl?"

"Fine," he said. "I need to patrol my other stations anyhow. Talk to you later."

"OK, thanks," Crimson said, calming briefly, but the anxiety was still there.

TIME CREPT ON, and Crimson looked down the tunnel, and checked on Covelli every few minutes. Several previously unnoticed dens lined the tunnel. When she came with Labrad, her mind had been too occupied. A strong scent of Norterridane was in several of them. Perhaps warriors slept here while on duty even though the dens were mostly unusable. In fact, the den Covelli slept in was damp.

A strong and nauseating smell came through the den opposite where Crimson and Covelli waited. It smelled of rotting flesh, reminding Crimson of the first time she had come across that scent. *A cave lizard.*

Crimson could not move, paralyzed by the memory of the creature that had almost killed her mother and her dragons. Her legs shook, and her tail tucked between her legs. Then she saw a bony, clawed hand coming over the opening in the den's ceiling. A snake tongue flashed for a moment, then was gone, followed by a hissing voice ...

"Dragons ..."

It crawled halfway out into the den. A terrified squeal brought Crimson out of the trance. Covelli backed away toward the cave wall. Crimson lit her claws with blue fire, and the cave lizard paused. Its tongue flickered out of its bony mouth, and yellow eyes focused on Crimson.

Without warning, the den wall shattered, hurling rocks and dirt at Crimson. She yelped as a rock slammed into her nose. The fire from her claws vanished and the cave lizard rushed forward.

Crimson called on the magic fire again, this time creating an arc of flames. The lizard darted to the left, fire scorching a small part of its leg. The skin bubbled from the heat. Its large bony tail whipped around, smashing into the den wall near Crimson.

Fierce growls filled the tunnel. The warriors must have smelled the lizard. The lizard whipped its head around, facing its new foe.

Crimson called an arc of fire once again, burning the lizard's exposed side. The lizard backed into the den whence it had come, and a pack of Norterridane followed.

Beryl was among them. The growling and fighting lasted only minutes.

"Crimson, what are you doing here? You know you're not supposed to bring your dragon to the Underground," Beryl scolded, closing the gap between them. "Cave lizards love the scent of dragons; the less we have here, the better."

"I was looking for you. It's important." Crimson knew the rules, but hadn't the Elders just brought her to the Underground days before?

"What could be more important than protecting your dragon?"

"I saw Azuran."

Beryl stopped in his tracks, jaw clenched and muscles tense. "You saw Azuran again? Where? Was he alone?"

A Norterridane came out from the den with the dead cave lizard. "We will need some help to move the body into the lake. I am going to get some now."

"Good," Beryl replied.

Crimson didn't know how Beryl felt about Azuran, or about any dragon for that matter. He definitely didn't seem happy.

"Was that the important news?" He said.

"He is working with the serpents to find some sort

of power. Some powerful magic that is hidden in Crystal Lake, and whatever it is, I felt it."

"The Elders thought the serpents might still be around. How many are there?"

"I don't know."

"What is this power?"

"I don't know. Azuran thought I would know, and I think he is hoping I will find out or find a way to get it."

"I will let the Elders know at once. Take the dragon back to the reeds." Beryl turned and started up the tunnel.

"That's not all. He is growing tusks," Crimson said.

"How is that possible?" He said to himself.

"Maybe Bowen will have an idea."

"Bowen has gone back to Alannador. I have no idea how serpents and dragons sharing power works. But certainly, magic mixing could be causing Azuran to be turning. But it is nothing I have ever heard of."

Bowen left? It was so soon; her father had just come back. Crimson couldn't think of that now.

"Maybe it's … some sort of … spell or something," Crimson said.

"We know so little about serpents. All we have ever known is they kill dragons."

"But they are not killing them anymore," Crimson said. "They kept Azuran alive, and they let the hatchlings go."

"It doesn't seem like their nature at all," Beryl said.

"Maybe the dragons haven't told us everything," Crimson said, and she began to question what exactly they had gotten themselves into protecting dragons.

"The Elders know more, I am certain," Beryl said, walking over to Covelli, who was still huddled near the back wall of the den. He placed his paw on Covelli's scales. "She looks a little pale. Like a dull turquoise color. She needs to be back in the water soon. That much I do know about dragons."

Crimson summoned the dragon magic and snuggled up with Covelli to comfort her. "The lizard is dead. It won't hurt you."

"You must take her home," Beryl said, and he led them to the edge of the Underground tunnel, where the water level began. Covelli splashed in, staying close to Crimson.

"If Azuran doesn't come back to the lake, we should look for him. We have to save him," Crimson said to Beryl.

"And get ourselves killed?" Beryl said, looking at a scar on his side. "We barely survived the last two run-ins with the serpents, and that's only because there were enough dragons around to use that formidable power of yours."

"I know, but …"

"But what? It's better to let the Elders and warriors handle this. I would love the chance to charge into battle again and kill those monsters, but we must do it the right way. We don't even know where he is, or if he is with the Schorl."

"We are dragon keepers, right? So we need to save Azuran, or at least see if he needs to be saved," Crimson said.

"I don't know if you are supposed to save him," Beryl said. He sat at the edge of the tunnel. He didn't speak for quite some time. He just sat there, his eyes scrunched and his muzzle tense. "I don't know if we are supposed to save him."

In the silent moment, Crimson could hear movement in the tunnel. The warriors were on their way back.

"Do you think he was looking for you, or was it by chance he was at the lake?"

"I think he was looking for me and Covelli."

"The serpents may be wary of your power. Be careful, Crimson. I know the Elders do not want an

Obsidian as an enemy, but it is not up to you to save him."

"Are we going to try?" Crimson asked, trying to piece together what this all meant.

"If the Elders approve," Beryl said, then added, "If they do let us look for him, you cannot go."

"Of course," Crimson said, watching Covelli chase after small minnows in the entryway. "My first duty is to my dragon. He seemed so different than when he was a hatchling."

"He grew up with serpents; of course, he's not the same. Where did he go after he spoke with you?"

"He flew off toward the eastern Black Mountains and Mount Xenoti."

Warriors pulled the dead cave lizard out of the tunnel, jaws clamped down on the skin of the foul beast. They dug their paws into the ground, and though there were many, it was difficult for them to move the large corpse.

"I will let the Elders know," Beryl said, rubbing his nose with his paw. "Now get Covelli out of here. We do not want her dragon scent attracting more cave lizards. We cannot afford more battles right now, and I cannot stand the smell of that dead one."

"You're right," Crimson said, her stomach still turning from the lizard odor.

CRIMSON paced back and forth outside her small den. She waited to hear what the Elders had told Beryl. What were they going to do? Were they going to find Azuran and bring him back?

"Crimson, stop and concentrate," Amber said, dropping the magic stone at her paws.

"I don't know if I can."

"Lots on your mind; believe me, I know. What you did with that fire was … It was more power than this stone, that's for sure, but I am ordered to teach you Magi magic, so you need to learn."

Crimson sat down and placed her claws on the stone, feeling for that glimpse of magic. She was used to feeling waves of magic. Finding magic in stone was like reaching for a dragon power that was far away. She imagined pulling it out of the stone and into her paw. A flicker of magic moved from the stone into her claw.

"What do I do now?" she said, tail wagging.

"Now place it back in the stone. After you do that a few times, I will show you how to manipulate some elements."

Crimson attempted to pull magic from the stone a few more times, to no avail.

"I can't think about it now," she said.

"I will come back tomorrow. Perhaps by then you will have gotten the news you are looking for."

Crimson looked down at Covelli, who was rolling in the mud and snapping at flies and the insects near the reeds. Did she worry about Azuran?

The wait for news seemed unbearable. Crimson paced again. Covelli fidgeted as well; then she cried out in her high-pitched dragon sounds.

"I am sorry, Covelli. I must be making you worried. I just can't help but think of Azuran all alone out there. I know you just met him, but you didn't know him. He was wonderful and brave. I failed him. I thought he was dead, and we just left. I should have looked for him. If only I had been stronger."

She rubbed her paw on Covelli's scales. It looked odd, red fur against turquoise scales.

"When I thought he'd died, I swore to be the greatest dragon keeper that ever lived. I can't fail him again. I just can't."

The young dragon moved closer and rubbed her soft scales onto Crimson's fur. Crimson sat down on the muddy ground and brushed her paw on the dragon's back. The scales were still wet from the last swim. Crimson summoned the dragon's power, connecting with her and calming her.

"I know that no one can understand this. I don't think he fought with the serpents of his own free will."

Covelli brushed her forefoot on Crimson's fur. Crimson looked down on her fondly. "I haven't been the best keeper to you either. That's it! No more worrying about Azuran. Let's go get something to eat."

Still Crimson's mind was on Azuran. He seemed so different. But how much did any of them actually know about dragons?

Covelli caught a fish without any effort at all. Crimson remembered how long it took to teach Chalcedony and Azuran to fish; sea dragons were naturals. Crimson pulled her fish from the barbed hooks on her claws and chewed through the fish scales to the delicious meat.

The reeds rustled, and a tan-and-sable head appeared in the reeds to the right. Crimson wondered if she would ever get used to the deep scar across his muzzle. He had healed rather well for someone who had almost died. Azuran would have killed Midnight had Torbern not jumped in the way.

Torbern and Crimson rubbed shoulders in greeting.

"Torbern, where's Beryl? What did they say? Are they going after Azuran?"

"They aren't sending anyone."

"Why?"

"He said it would be dangerous to send someone out there, especially with cave lizards being more abundant and attacking. We have fortified many of the walls in the lower tunnels, but it really only slows them down."

Crimson glared at him, heat rising in her body. Her nose crinkled. "They're just going to leave Azuran out there alone?" she barked.

"Whoa, I am just the messenger," he replied, stepping back. "Besides, he is a mature dragon; I am sure he's fine. As long as he doesn't pose a threat to the Underground, Ferruginous says we shouldn't have any dealings with him. Jet is out searching for him and will find out what we need to know. Norterridane do not need to be part of it."

"Why not?" Crimson said, her curiosity calming her anger.

"Serpents are evil. That dragon has lived with them and fought with them."

"That dragon has a name."

"That dragon almost killed me … and Midnight."

"Do you think I've forgotten?" she barked.

Covelli hissed at Torbern protectively, lurching forward.

Crimson and Torbern exploded with laughter.

"I have not forgotten," Crimson said, her voice soft. The horror of that day replayed in her mind. Blood gushing from Midnight's wounds, and the serpent coming to kill Chalcedony. At that moment, she believed they were all going to die. She would never forget, and she wouldn't forget that Azuran had tried to attack Amber. "You don't understand."

"Yes, I do. I know dragons are like our pups, and I have never been a keeper, so I cannot speak of the magic bond, but I hear it is powerful," he said, his voice forgiving, calming, and seemingly sincere. He moved by her side and gave a loving lick on her muzzle. "But if you really wanted my opinion, we wouldn't be keeping dragons anymore."

"What?" Crimson couldn't believe he had said that. How many others felt that way? Her dad felt so strongly that protecting dragons was what they needed to do.

"The Elders believe that Azuran shared his magic with the serpents. They believe he did it willingly, since he attacked Norterridane. The serpents are going to try to get that magic, and we have to prepare. You said he is growing tusks, and they believe he is turning into a serpent—if he is not a serpent already. I do understand where you are coming from, but there is nothing you or I can do," Torbern said.

A stabbing pain jabbed her heart. How could words hurt so much? She understood why they would think that way, but there must some other explanation. He wasn't evil.

Crimson let out a deep sigh. "You're wrong. There is something I can do. I can find him and convince him to fly to Alannador with the other dragons."

"Don't be stupid."

"I'm not. I am being reasonable," she replied.

"Look," Torbern said. "Just take care of Covelli.

Be a good keeper, and let the warriors deal with the serpents."

When Torbern moved out of sight, she turned and nudged Covelli, who had lain down for a nap. The dragon yawned and curled into a tighter ball.

"Fine, you can sleep," Crimson whispered, "but when you wake up, we will find Azuran. Chalcedony and Azuran traveled all the way to the willows with me when they were as small as you, and we made it. We will travel upriver to the mountains and bring Azuran back."

Raindrops settled on Crimson's fur and on the ground. They splattered on an uneaten fish that lay on the ground, and they splattered on Covelli, who lay next to it. The dragon must have been exhausted from the visit to the crevasse. Crimson recalled when Chalcedony had become ill. It turned out she was maturing and shedding her skin. But Covelli was nowhere near that age. She hoped she just needed more rest and would eat in a few hours. She pushed Covelli into the lake water and lay beside her. It wasn't the safest thing to do, but Covelli would need water to keep her scales moist when the rain stopped.

She rested beside the dragon, and small waves from the lake gently lapped against the sand, keeping her red fur wet. She pawed mud on the dragon and sniffed the air; wet dirt and rain, nothing more. All was peaceful and calm. She closed her eyes and fell asleep.

CHAPTER 13

MALACHITE Stood on a mountain peak near Xenoti. He looked down over the lake. It seemed small from this high up. The Obsidian dragons were keeping watch somewhere over the city. How he hated those Obsidians, but now he knew they had a weakness. He also knew that the older dragons were much stronger than Azuran. He suddenly realized how powerful Azuran would become and wondered if Onixian would share in that power. He would have to make sure the dragon was on their side.

"Hesson is patrolling the western mountains, as ordered. We should know more soon," Andalus said, walking by.

"Good news," Malachite said. "The Obsidian

seems to be following a particular patrol path and should be easy to avoid."

"What can we do now?" Andalus said. "Azuran couldn't get to the magic?"

"I never told him to try and get it. I told him to find out more about it. His headstrong ways are influenced by Onixian for sure."

"Maybe he can still find out information."

Malachite looked up at the massive serpent, glad to have his loyalty. "Perhaps it would be easier if he does, but I always have a backup plan."

"What? We can't get within five hundred wings of their home; the dragon will kill us."

"Flying, yes; swimming, no. I have seen a river that leads from the mountain to the lake. We will follow the river and swim to the depths of the lake. The magic stone may be easy to retrieve. Dragons cannot hold their breath as we can."

"The lake cannot be very deep," Andalus agreed. "When do we leave?"

"As soon as Fairburn lands," Malachite said, looking over his shoulder at the stone-reader approaching. Malachite had much respect for her and thought perhaps one day she would rule by his side as queen. While Schorl normally did not share in such power, he would not mind sharing the world with her.

The three serpents walked down the mountainside and to the edge of a stream. The water was slightly warm, coming from the heated depths of the earth near the volcano. The water was shallow, only coming up to Malachite's shin. They were fortunate that a river flowed from this side of the mountain. It came from a hot spring underground and cooled as it went down the mountain to Crystal Lake. Malachite slurped up the water.

"We can only hope it deepens before reaching the lake," Malachite said, walking downstream with the river water rushing past his feet. They walked swiftly scanning the terrain.

The river deepened, but not enough to completely cover the serpents' hunched bodies, so the progress was slow. They stopped often and scanned the area for potential threats. The water deepened further. Small fish swam against the current, attempting to swim upriver, to no avail. Each one eventually followed the stream. Older fish would jump the rapids to the warm spawning grounds near the top of the spring.

Luck stayed with them as they reached the lake's edge. Reeds and grasses grew tall on the lakeshore, and hills blocked the view on both sides of the river. Malachite grinned; then he heard a warning bark.

He leapt out of the river in the direction of the sound. He ran, his large feet smashing the grass as he went. He could not let himself slow down; the Norterridane could not return to warn any others. His eyes scanned the grass as he ran, catching the slightest movement. The Norterridane dashed to the left and Malachite jumped. He grabbed it by the neck and quickly snapped it before turning to find the rest of the pack. They always traveled in packs. Andalus and Fairburn followed. Fairburn grabbed another two with her right arms and stabbed them in the heart. Within a few short moments, the pack was dead.

"Are you not worried about other Norterridane searching for the pack? No doubt they will notice their absence," Fairburn asked.

"We are far from the city; it would have taken a while for the patrol to return. We will be gone before they come to search, and they will not find any bodies." Malachite grinned again.

The serpents ate a quick and satisfying meal before returning to the water.

"We must be careful in the lake; they fish there," Fairburn said.

"I didn't see any Norterridane when Andalus and I climbed the hills. They fish close to their home, not the far side of the lake. We will go deep in the lake, far below where they are able to swim."

They swam down deep into the water. The stone in Fairburn's hand glowed, guiding the way to the deep crevasse at the bottom of the lake. It was wide and dark. Malachite waved his hand, signaling for Fairburn to hand him the stone. It glowed brightly compared to the darkness of the lake. Andalus stood lookout as Malachite descended farther into the crevasse, his arms grabbing at layers of mud along the walls. Mud turned to harder stone the farther he went. All that lay ahead was darkness, but the stone glowed brighter as he descended. Still the crevasse seemed to go deeper. Along each side of the crevasse was not soft sediment but solid stone. Malachite clawed the surface. His red claws barely made a scratch. These stones seemed to be fortified with magic.

He clawed until he felt the pressure building in his lungs. He turned and swam back up to the top of the lake. Reaching the surface, he gasped in the cool, refreshing air. He had not intended to be under the water that long, and still he had not reached the source of power. His forked tongue caught the scent of wet Norterridane. He scanned the lake. In the distance, he could see Norterridane diving and swimming in the lake. They swam upwind, so he knew they had not yet caught his scent. He sank underwater. Locating Andalus and Fairburn, he swam back to the river.

"How can we get the power?" he asked Fairburn. "The stone glowed brighter the deeper I went, but the crevasse seems to go to the depths of the earth, with sides of stone."

"We need more information."

"It looks like we must wait for Azuran after all," Malachite snarled.

"We have waited decades on Calimdural. What is waiting a little longer?" Fairburn said.

"You are wise," Malachite said, and opened his large wings. He flew back to the ice-covered mountains that were now his home.

MALACHITE SAT in his icy cave, going over ideas about how to get to the power in the lake. His claws scraped along the deer bones on the floor.

A shadow crept over the entrance. Hesson's large wedge-shaped head peered in. "My king, Azuran has returned."

Malachite walked out of the cave, placing his

claws on Hesson's shoulder. Azuran and Onixian approached from the south.

"Azuran, it seems you have a chance to redeem yourself," Malachite called, stretching his wings and meeting Azuran in the snow. "We must find out more about this Norterridane. How long do you think it will take for her to divulge the secrets of her power?"

"After what happened at the lake, who knows."

"You must go to her and gain her trust. I have a feeling her power is the key. You said she sensed the power behind the stone. She could locate it."

"Perhaps there is another way. If we can get dragon eggs and gain more power. Perhaps a sea dragon of our own—" Hesson said.

"That would take forever," Onixian said.

"You just want all the power for yourself," Hesson said, stepping toward Onixian aggressively. Onixian met him head-on, and they clashed, tusks interlocked.

"Enough!" Malachite said, pulling them apart. Serpents were always fighting, a magic-craving effect.

Hesson backed away, breathing heavily and growling. Onixian was much more relaxed, as if the attack hadn't fazed him.

Malachite rubbed his claws along his tusks.

"Azuran, I will give you till the next full moon. If you do not have something by then, we kill the Norterridane and take her dragon."

Onixian smiled wide. "I would love the challenge."

"Then it shall be yours," Malachite said, then turned and went back into his den. He wondered if the magic the canine possessed could be transferred to a serpent. If it could, perhaps he should be the one to do it. He moved back into his den and clawed away at the ice and stone, piece by piece, trying to find the next steps that would bring him more power.

CHAPTER 14

THE reeds rustled. The dragon moved slightly but did not wake. The stars shone dimly in the night sky as the first rays of light spread across the land. The scents of reeds, algae, sand, and water drifted near. A familiar scent was on the air, and it lifted her heart immediately. Crimson left Covelli's side.

"Midnight!"

Crimson wagged her tail and moved to the reeds to meet him, trudging gently over the muddy ground. Midnight had been her advisor when she first had found Azuran and Chalcedony, and her friend through the battle with the serpents. When he was gravely injured, Crimson feared she would lose him forever, but now he was out of the Underground. Her heart danced.

"Hey," Midnight said, licking Crimson's snout and rubbing up against her shoulder. His eyes sparkled in the starlight, and his black fur blended almost completely with the darkness. Even with Crimson's keen sight, he remained partially hidden until he was right next to her.

"How are you?" Crimson said. "Are you feeling better?"

"Yeah. Just muscle cramps if I do too much."

Midnight sat by Covelli, tilting an ear in toward the sleeping dragon. "It seems like forever ago we were living in the red willows, raising three dragons."

"Torbern told me what happened. I came to see if you were OK."

"Yeah, I know." Crimson sighed. "They aren't going to send anyone to help Azuran."

"I'm sorry."

"I thought dragon keepers were supposed to be alone," she teased.

"It seems you are the exception. The Elders let me come to make sure you weren't doing something rash."

"Like going and finding Azuran?"

"You gotta let the Elders take care of this."

Crimson looked up at all of the stars. "Do you think all the dragons are up there?"

"I don't know. What would they do in the stars?" Midnight said.

"Maybe fly around the universe."

"I prefer the wind," Midnight said.

Every Norterridane knew the story of life and death. When Norterridane died, they were met by their great ancestor, Mawto. The creator of life. All Norterridane ran with the wind, through the forest and over the mountains, wild and free with their pack, waiting to return to the world again in another life. Crimson liked to think all the lost warriors of the past were running with her when she ran through the forest, or swimming beside her as she swam.

"I really thought you had died that day on the battlefield," Crimson said after a moment.

"Yeah, I thought I was going to."

Midnight moved next to Crimson and she leaned against his shoulder.

"Torbern has been promoted to pack leader," Midnight said.

"That is good news. Right?"

"Of course it is. It is just that I had been hoping to lead a pack. But with my injury it is not possible."

"You just have to give it time," Crimson said,

encouraging her friend. "You know, I was actually thinking about going to look for Azuran. We could convince him to stay with us or go to Alannador."

"You're not going to let it go, are you?"

"He needs our help. I just know it."

"There is a war going on. In war there are casualties. Maybe Azuran is one of them."

"He is not dead."

"I know; I mean he is one of the serpents."

Crimson looked off again into the sky. The sun had risen, and streaks of light peaked through the reeds.

"I know you think you owe Azuran something because you didn't save him. I know how hard it was for you when he fell over the waterfall. It took a long time for you to heal. But you can't keep blaming yourself. No one could have stopped the serpent," Midnight said.

"I could have, if I had known about my powers."

"But you didn't know. Now look at who Azuran is now. Why was he asking about mysterious powers?"

"I went to see what the power was. I didn't know what I would do if I found it. But Azuran can't get it; it's too far down."

"The Elders will take care of that too," Midnight

said, then looked at the sleeping dragon by the lake. "How long has she been sleeping like that?"

"Like what?" Crimson nudged Covelli. The dragon barely moved. Covelli's scales were paler in color than they had ever been. A gooey slime substance ran from her nose, making it hard for her to breathe. Her eyes were cloudy, and her gills appeared to be clogged with the slimy substance. Difficult, labored air moved with each breath, and Crimson had to do something. She had to get her to the Magi before she got worse.

"Oh no."

"We need to get her to the Underground; something is wrong," Midnight said. "What did she eat?"

"Come on, Covelli, we have to swim to the Underground," Crimson said, pawing the dragon. Covelli twitched and stretched out her front legs slowly, as if she could barely lift them. "Fish … she just ate fish."

"She is definitely ill."

"Come on," Midnight said. "You will feel better when you are swimming. I promise."

The dragon nodded slowly. Crimson pushed her nose under the dragon's body and wriggled her head under, pushing the hatchling to her feet. She growled as she moved the dragon. *What good is it to keep dragons on our own?* This wasn't the first time she had questioned it. *Why not have a pack of Norterridane guarding dragons? Maybe someone else would have noticed sooner.*

Crimson pushed Covelli through the reeds and the deeper water. As it flowed over her, Covelli began to move. But she seemed disoriented. Crimson swam along one side, and Midnight swam along the other, taking turns surfacing for air and then swimming back down near the dragon, who used one wing more than the other to swim in a lopsided manner. It was because of whatever illness this was. *Could it be something she ate? Some fish with poison? The snails she played with? Impossible. A fish allergy? Perhaps, but why now?*

Every moment seemed to drag on. Crimson knew they had to make it to the Underground. The Magi were her only hope. The slow progress increased her fear. The dragon might not make it. She tried to be positive, but thoughts of Covelli dying kept entering her mind. Whatever it was, she had gotten ill so quickly, without warning. It would have been faster to use dragon magic to call gills and swim beside her without resurfacing, but she dared not drain Covelli's power now.

A warm dragon power pulled at her senses, at the tip of her mind, asking her to call upon it. *Azuran?*

The Obsidian dragon landed in the water beside her. He studied the struggling dragon.

"What's wrong with her?" he said.

"I am not sure. I have to get her to the Underground. Help us, please."

Azuran closed his talons around the hatchling.

"Where to?"

"It's an underwater entrance. I'll guide you."

Crimson took a deep breath and dove into the lake. She swam quickly, looking back only to see that Azuran still followed and Midnight followed. He was keeping up a good pace. He hadn't been the best swimmer when he was young, but he used his wings to help boost himself through the water.

Up ahead was the tunnel. Crimson swam up ahead and climbed up out of the water. Azuran could fit his head, neck, and right front foot in, but his wings, even closed, were much too large. He set Covelli gently on the ground.

"This is as far as I can go."

"Thank you, Azuran. I will not forget what you have done," Crimson said, giving him a gentle nudge with her nose.

Covelli moved slowly over the damp den floor.

"Come on, Covelli," Crimson said, pushing her to her feet. Azuran disappeared back through the watery entrance, and Midnight climbed in the tunnel opening.

"Keep her moving," he said.

Crimson guided the dragon to the rim of the tunnel, nudging Covelli gently with her nose to help her up. Covelli wheezed and coughed. Greenish-yellow slime flew out of her mouth, but more slime oozed out of her nostrils and gills, blocking her airways. The dragon collapsed on the ground, mouth open, breathing in as much air as she could. Crimson had to leave her. She moved through the tunnel and howled.

A few warriors moved out of guard tunnels. "What is it?"

"My dragon; she is sick. I think she is dying."

One of the warriors ran down the tunnel as fast as he could.

"He'll get the healer. Show me the dragon," the other warrior said.

Crimson ran with him back to where Covelli and Midnight were lying.

"The Magi will be here soon; Amber's den is not far away. I will help keep guard here with you," the warrior said.

"Thank you," Crimson said.

"It's my pleasure," he said, and picked up his ears and snout, alert to the sounds and smells in the cave and the watery entrance. Crimson listened as well, hoping another cave lizard wouldn't come through the tunnels now.

Covelli lay still. The only sign she lived was the slow heaving of her chest. Crimson paced the width of the tunnel while intermittently checking that the dragon was still breathing. Paw steps echoed through the tunnel, and the scent of the Magi entered Crimson's nose.

Amber dropped a small, slightly glowing stone onto the ground next to Covelli. Amber examined her body, touching a few of her scales with her paw. She delicately lifted a cloudy white substance from the dragon's eye. She placed one paw on her chest and scratched a symbol into the stone, then placed her paw on the tiny stone, so small that it was completely covered by her dark fur. The paw on the stone glowed slightly for a moment, then the paw on Covelli's chest. The dragon's chest rose and fell with ease now, but the dragon did not move.

"Is she going to be OK?" Midnight said.

"I have opened the airways temporarily, but it will not be enough. Her scales are dry and flaky, her eyes clouded, and her organs are failing. We need to make a pool in the Magi den for her. We need more magic stones, or your dragon will die. We must quarantine her in the Magi den; there is not much time. Keep all dragons out of the city."

"What is wrong with her?" Crimson gasped, heart pounding in her chest.

"Send for Beryl and Ferruginous. She has contracted the dragon plague."

CHAPTER 15

BERYL stood at the edge of the warrior den. The chief guard's proud face softened as he spoke. "Mica, take your pack and the explorers to the aspen forest to look for magic stones."

"What about this magic in the lake? Could it be a stone?" Mica said.

"We have no way to reach it and no way to know."

Mica nodded.

"Earlier I sent several packs to other locations on Genorrdia to search for the magic stones. We do not normally patrol past the cliffs, but we must. There are fewer and fewer magic stones available. I am entrusting your pack."

"It's risky; the only keeper who ever went to the forest was killed by serpents," Mica said.

"Odds are that they are somewhere in the mountains with Azuran, but if some are near the forest, we still have to take that chance."

"Can I please go, Beryl?" Crimson pleaded. "I can't just sit here doing nothing and watching Covelli die."

Beryl stood for a moment in deep thought.

"OK, but Mica is the alpha. If you disobey any of her orders, there will be consequences."

"I understand," Crimson said, letting out the deep breath of air she had been holding as he decided.

"It will take a day to reach the cliffs near the Crystal River and navigate down the sloping sand hills of the wasteland. That leaves us only one day to search and make it back in time," Mica said.

Crimson's heart sank. "Is that enough time?" Her words were ignored as the pack prepared to leave. Mica sent a runner to call the explorer, a Norterridane who had a knack for sensing magic stones, though they could not use the magic.

"Good luck," Beryl said. He turned abruptly and walked out of the warrior den.

A SHORT TIME LATER, Crimson, Mica, ten warriors, and a stone explorer bounded across the grassy hills near Crystal Lake. They moved swiftly, staying in pack formation. Chato, the explorer, took the lead. His fur was light tan and he had darker brown pointed ears. He reminded Crimson of Torbern, though Torbern's color pattern was darker and Chato's snout was longer. Chato ran with his head down, whipping his nose back and forth, sniffing and searching.

Crimson ran at a quickened pace to keep up. *What smell does he search for?* Crimson could differentiate many scents—dragons, Jasperillian, and even different types of rock and soil—but magic rocks smelled no different to her. Even when Amber drew power from the stone in training, she for sure would have noticed a different smell then.

The pack ran over the hills along the Crystal River toward the sandy wasteland. The cliffs stretched almost the entire length of Genorrdia. A sloping sand dune was the only safe way around the cliffs on this side of the plateau. The other way Crimson had learned was a hidden path under the waterfall of the Sapphire River. It was obscured on the cliffside. She had travelled there with Midnight and Torbern on her way back from the abandoned cave-dweller caves, but that would take much too long. Soon they left the river and ran though grasslands. They moved urgently, ignoring animals and insects that were normally a distraction. Each Norterridane knew the mission, and what was at stake.

The sun was far past the midday mark in the sky when they reached the cliffs. Chato led the pack through the grasses, close but not too close to the drop-off. The ground leveled out and sloped sharply down into the sandy land.

Mica signaled for the pack to rest. They lay down, hidden in the grasses.

"Nothing yet," Chato said to Mica, panting heavily.

"We hadn't expected there would be. Rest now, friend; we have a long journey ahead." She placed her head briefly over his, signaling affection and leadership at the same time.

Mica checked on each member of the pack before she lay down to rest herself. Crimson could tell she was a good leader, and it was her responsibly to care for the pack.

"How are you holding up?" Mica asked Crimson.

"I am doing OK," she replied. Mica turned to leave.

Crimson respected Mica as an alpha. They had

once been friends when they were younger, and fought together in battle, but that seemed like a different life. "What is it Chato is looking for?"

"He is looking for scents of magic. It may seem like a wild goose chase, but explorers have a heightened sense of smell. They can smell things farther away and deeper underground than we can. That is why an explorer is part of every pack. Though they are not bound to one pack in particular."

"He is our best chance of helping Covelli."

"He is the only chance. We would never smell the magic stones, and even if you could see the glow, most are buried, and we have to dig them out."

"You have hunted for stones before?"

"Yes," Mica replied. "Pack life is very different from keeping dragons."

Crimson was not sure what Mica meant by that. Mica had never wanted to become a dragon keeper. Did she think dragon keeping was less important than being a pack warrior?

Crimson walked into a small patch of grass and lay down to rest. The soft grass tickled her paws. The pain of the day overtook her. Her legs ached, and they would have to move on again soon. Her mind drifted to thoughts of Covelli.

A short time later, the pack was on the move, gracefully and swiftly navigating the terrain.

THE SAND BURNED at their feet as they dashed through the wasteland. They only passed through a small portion, but it would be grueling if they did not pass in twilight. Darkness would not help, as the desert creatures came out at that time, and many were poisonous.

"Keep up the pace," Mica ordered. "Let's get out of here as soon as we can."

The dry grassland soil was a welcome sight to all the Norterridane. Whimpers could be heard from even the toughest warriors. They had moved almost nonstop the rest of the day. "Let's set up a perimeter and get some sleep."

"Not yet," Chato said. "I smell something up ahead, farther into the grasses."

The pack followed Chato into taller grasses. The grasses came up past Crimson's shoulder and tickled her nose.

Chato and a few of the pack dug into the ground. He stuck his nose in the ground and closed his eyes.

His lifted his head and shook off the dirt. "There is a stone here."

He dug until he unearthed a small black stone. A light glow emanated from it.

He found it! Relieved, Crimson sat down in the grass.

"We can go now," Mica said.

"No." Chato shook his head and turned the stone over in the dirt. "Its magic is almost gone and is fading. It is like a glow stone in its last hours, only it cannot be replenished by the sun."

"What does that mean?"

"We have to keep looking. The magic would not last the trip home."

Crimson sighed. *Of course it isn't that easy.*

"We will rest here a while and continue the search," Mica said.

Mica moved around to check on each member of the pack just as she had before.

Two betas moved away from the group to patrol, while the rest curled up in the grasses. Crimson thought of Covelli and the last image she had seen of the young dragon. She had been an awful shade of turquoise and barely breathing. She did not want to think of her that way. She wanted to think of her swimming freely in the lake and collecting snails to bring back to the den. She had not yet learned to translate Norterridane language. She was too young to die. Crimson stared at the magic stone, watching the glow gradually fade.

Slowly sleep found Crimson, but it was not a peaceful one.

The cold crept through the darkness, even before Crimson could see the snow. She shivered and searched for shapes in the gloom. She sniffed the air.

The white Norterridane appeared, filling the snow-filled darkness with a sudden bright light. Its beautiful silvery-white coat glistened in the light.

"Jasper?" Crimson called into the storm.

The Norterridane came closer to Crimson and looked down fondly upon her, like a mother does her pup, and nodded. Jasper opened her snout to speak. Crimson could not hear her words through the whistling of the storm. She raised her ears and leaned in. There was no sound, but somehow she knew what she wanted to tell her.

"Beware the dragon," she said, her voice chilling.

A tingle ran down Crimson's spine. A warning. "What dragon?"

"You must be prepared to challenge all you believe. Things are not as they seem."

Then Jasper moved forward through Crimson's

body, like wind rustling her fur. Wings fluttered in the distance. Two obsidian dragons flew by and a green dragon materialized on the edge of the lake, fuzzy and unclear as if shrouded by fog. Crimson turned as Jasper walked away in the distance.

"Jasper, wait," Crimson called. "What do you mean?"

The silvery-white coat moved farther and farther, and then disappeared, leaving the snowy blizzard and once again darkness.

A RUMBLING of thunder awakened the pack. Crimson opened her eyes. Mica and the pack crouched low and alert. They crept low in the grasses, ears perked in the direction of the sound, their fur hidden within the grasses and bushes. A dark tan Norterridane twitched her ears.

"Stay down," she whispered.

Crimson spread out her body and rolled over, preparing to run.

It was not thunder from the sky, but the ground. *A stampede.*

Still like a statue, Crimson crouched and watched the grassland.

Through the blades of grass, she saw them. Out of the clearing, rushing toward the forest, a herd of deer frantically raced, and bounded over the grass. Behind them a Schorl serpent hunted. Another moved alongside, then another, long legs moving them at such a speed they overtook the deer within seconds. One serpent bit off a deer's head. The other leapt and landed on a deer, crushing it under its weight. Another clawed at a deer with its six arms. It was a massacre. The deer had no chance. They were torn apart by the serpents. One by one, the serpents carried their kill into the aspen forest.

When the sounds of serpent footfalls could no longer be heard, Mica brought the pack together.

"The serpents did not abandon Genorrdia," Mica whispered. "We have to return to the Underground."

"We must find more stones. We have to save Covelli. If we don't return with stones, she will die," Crimson pleaded. If they left now, their journey would have been for nothing. *I have to convince Mica. I have to.*

"This is why dragon keepers usually do not venture farther than the plateau; much of Genorrdia still needs to be explored. The risk is great. The only keeper to live way south in the aspen forest is dead and so is his dragon because of the serpents. We cannot afford to be here now."

"The serpents are gone. We could search the area," Chato said.

"It is no longer up to us," Mica said. "We cannot be certain the next stone will even have magic. Chato, you said something has drained the stones. We can only hope that one of the other groups was successful. Let's go, before the serpents return."

"We are leaving now?" Crimson whimpered.

"There is nothing we can do. We must leave before they smell us. We cannot search the aspen forest with serpents about. We have no armor. We are but a pack of twelve. Even if we could kill one, there were at least twenty serpents. There is no way we could win, and the Elders must know."

"Didn't you see how they tore the deer apart? Do you want them to kill us all?" A warrior said.

"But I have magic," Crimson protested. Her legs were weak, and it took all her strength to stand.

"How much could your fire claws do now? No dragons are near. You could burn a few, but twenty? It would only be a matter of time before you were killed as well," Mica growled. "Face it, Crimson, there is nothing we can do."

She turned, and with a swing of her tail, she

signaled for the pack to move back the way they had come.

Crimson's breath came fast, her jaw trembled, and she backed away from Mica and the pack. Her eyes blurred as the tears came and fell upon her fur. There was nothing she could do.

Covelli would die.

THE journey back was an unpleasant one. Crimson wanted to run and look for the stones herself, but she had no idea how to find any. Plus, she didn't really know how to use the stones. She felt helpless, and it was not a feeling she wanted to have. Rain began to pour, and thunder cracked in the sky, making her mood even worse.

For a moment the rain stopped. The Norterridane looked into the sky. A large shape flew overhead, blocking the droplets of water. The dragon landed a few paws away, its tusks oddly placed against glassy back scales.

Mica howled, and the pack moved into a battle formation. A blue eye turned toward the group, and the dragon moved closer. Crimson relaxed. "Mica, it's OK, it is Azuran."

Mica did not stand down, the fur on her rump was ruffled, and her ears flattened, teeth bared. The pack was also on alert, moving into attack formation. Though they all knew if the dragon attacked, they would all be dead.

"I'll talk to him," Crimson said, and moved away from the pack, not waiting for permission.

"Azuran, I'm glad you came back. I was worried about you. What are you doing here?"

Azuran calmly licked blood from a fresh kill off his claws before the rain washed it away.

"I wanted to find you. I've thought a lot about what happened last time. I overreacted, and I want to convince you to help me. Why are you away from the lake?"

"We came to look for magic stones. Covelli is very ill. She has the dragon plague."

"The weak often die of illness," Azuran said.

Crimson ignored his callous remark; she had seen worry flash briefly in his eyes.

"The dragon plague is different. If you had caught it as a hatchling, you would have died, and your sister."

"How did she get it?" Azuran said, placing his claw on his chin.

"We don't know."

"Do you think I got it from her?" Azuran said. A look of terror flashed over his face. "When I helped her?"

"We have no time to waste here," Mica said.

"We must be getting back to the Underground, if only to say goodbye to the—"

"And because of your serpent friends in the forest, we could not find the magic stones to save a dying dragon," Mica interjected, fur still raised on her back and teeth bared.

Azuran turned a curious blue eye her way. He moved his head closer, smelling her. "Such fire in such a small creature," he said, and it seemed he admired her. "Maybe I can help."

Crimson thought he sounded a lot like Onixian. Was he acting that way because of the pack?

"Why would you help us?" Mica sneered

"Why not? Crimson protected me when I was young, and Covelli is my kin. And if the plague gets to me, I know helping Covelli and Crimson would help me."

"He has a point," Chato said.

"Seems a convenient time," Mica said.

"I also need help with something, and if I help you, you owe me a favor. If there is nothing else I have learned from watching your kind, it is that you are loyal, and most loyal creatures are also honest."

"Unlike serpents," Mica growled.

"Yes, unlike serpents," the dragon agreed, spreading his wings wide, making a shield from the pouring rain. Mica relaxed slightly but was still on guard.

"How could you help us?" Crimson asked, moving closer to Azuran. His large body towered over the pack.

"I could take you to find the stones. The serpents will not be a problem."

Hope renewed in Crimson's heart. *Torbern and the Elders were wrong; he isn't turning evil.*

"Even if we looked now, we have only a day left to return with the stones. There is no guarantee that we can find any at all," Chato said.

"What about Galena?" Crimson said, thinking of the Magi that had helped her find the cave-dweller ruins.

"What do you suggest?" Mica said.

"Azuran could fly us there in half a day, and return. She must know where magic stones are nearby her den. She had some there."

"That is a big chance you are taking," Mica said.

"Do we have your permission to go?" Chato asked Mica.

"First I want to know what the dragon wants in return," the pack leader said.

"I want Crimson to help me find out what the magic is under the lake."

"And what are you going to do with it? Give it to the serpents?"

Azuran smiled. "No, I am not going to give it to any serpent."

His expression with his tusks gave him a shocking resemblance to the serpents, similar to when Onixian had smiled planning Crimson's death. She shook away any negative thoughts. He was here to help.

Mica moved to Crimson and spoke in Norterridane tongue. "This is not a good idea. We do not know what magic is under the lake."

"Mica, he can speak in both our tongue and the common one, so no point in trying to hide our intentions. We can talk to the Elders when we return. Right now, Azuran is the best chance of saving Covelli."

Mica looked at Crimson with concern. "We are almost to the city. I will inform the Elders and let you know what they say."

AZURAN LIFTED Crimson and Chato into the air. held them close to his chest. His claws were not quite big enough to carry them in his claws alone, but he was still growing. Relieved, Crimson relaxed. She had a chance to help Covelli, and perhaps a chance to help Azuran find his way back home.

Crimson shifted uncomfortably as the dragon scales rubbed against her fur and skin. It felt like stone rubbing against her body. Crimson tried to stay still, and as comfortable as she could.

They flew over the grasslands at a tremendous speed. Past the rain clouds and past the grassland. The air chilled Crimson's wet fur. She watched as the ground blurred beneath them. Indistinct greens with browns and soon a light blue. It took a second to register that the blue was the Little Blue River. The dragon did not pause when he flew over the patch of red and brown that was the red willows. Crimson wondered how much he remembered, and why he was suddenly interested in her help. What did he think that magic was, and what did he want with it?

Azuran landed at the edge of a forest. Bushes with large thorns grew up out of the sand and dirt. Crimson had been here right after Azuran had fallen off the waterfall.

"THE SERPENTS HAVE DONE something to you. They made you forget. You need to come with me to the Elders. They could help you get to Alannador. They could save you."

"I did not forget. I remember you battling the river weasels. I remember you fighting Onixian."

Crimson felt weak. It was if he had slammed the wind from her body with his tail. He remembered her and hadn't come back. "Why did you stay with the serpents, then?"

"To survive, and there is a connection between Onixian and I. Like the one I had with you, but stronger."

"That is how he became invincible," Crimson said.

"You must tell me how it is that dragons share power? Perhaps there is a way to unshare it as well."

"I don't know. What about Midnight?" Crimson stopped. She probably shouldn't have mentioned him. She looked away from the dragon briefly. "He helped raise you and you tried to kill him."

"It was war," Azuran said. "He got in the way. He once told me dragons are fierce creatures, and that is what I have grown to be. He would be proud."

"I know the serpents would kill all of us if they had the chance," Crimson said.

"Killing your enemies does not make you evil."

"We must go," Chato said. "Where is Galena?"

The thorny forest was just as Crimson remembered. The sharp spines stabbed into her paws as she walked, making the journey slow. Azuran pushed through, smashing the thorns and making a path. He crouched and moved under thorn branches, breaking them with his tough scales as he moved.

"Let's get this over with," Azuran said, sticking out his tongue and tasting the air. "This way."

Crimson stared at his tongue. Had it always been like that? She couldn't remember. She was so new at dragon keeping that paying attention to his tongue had been the last thing on her mind. Was this another transformation?

Chato shrugged and ran after Azuran. "He is right. I smell both magic and Norterridane. The den is close."

"How did you call that wall of fire?" Azuran asked.

"I used your power to call it."

"Can all Norterridane do that?"

"No. Just me."

"So it was you who killed Sodal?"

"Who is Sodal?"

"A Schorl serpent with red-tipped tusks. The king's guard. You made the wall of white fire that killed him. Onixian said he just disappeared into ashes in seconds."

A low warning growl came from Chato, stopping her before she gave him more information. Azuran did not appear to notice that Chato had signaled her. Pack code had not been translated when the dragon had learned her language.

"Why do you think you are the only one?" Azuran asked.

"I'm not sure," Crimson said. She wanted to trust him. She wanted to tell him how much she had learned, but Chato reminded her that she shouldn't. After all, he only came to help because he wanted something.

CHATO MOVED ON AHEAD despite the thorns. "We are close."

Galena emerged from her den slowly. She was

much older now, with more wiry gray fur. Her steps were slow, but her voice was melodic and welcoming like before. "Crimson, welcome. I see you have brought friends."

"This is Chato and Azuran."

"Azuran? The dragon that died?"

"Yes, but he didn't die. It's a long story. He is here to help us. Covelli, my dragon, has gotten the plague. We need magic stones to help her."

"Dragon plague," she said, raising her brow. "How is that possible?"

"Could she have gotten it from Azuran?"

Galena turned to Azuran. "Why have you stayed on Genorrdia?"

"This is my home," the dragon responded, glaring at Crimson.

"Azuran, I am sorry. It is the only thing that makes sense. You were near her. You were the only one." Just as she said it, Crimson realized that Olivine had also been near Covelli in the Elders' cave. What if it wasn't because of Azuran? And Jasper had warned against a dragon. What if it was Olivine she should be wary of?

"Has Azuran been to Alannador?" Galena asked calmly.

"No," Azuran said. "I have never left Genorrdia.

"Then it could not have come from him," Galena said matter-of-factly.

"Then how?" Chato said

"Olivine?" Crimson said. "She was with her in the Elders' cave, but she never touched her."

"And your dragon was not around others?"

"No none."

"Then it had to transfer from Olivine. There is no other way."

Crimson thought back to the first meeting with Olivine in the Elders' cave. She had felt her power and Covelli's. It was as if their magic touched.

"I gave it to her," Crimson said, breathless. Her shoulders slumped.

"Perhaps," Galena said, walking to Crimson to comfort her in the realization. "Just as dragon parents used to pass the plague to their children, by sharing magic. But something bothers me about it. Something is off. Let the Elders know of this, and perhaps they can find the truth.

"But I thought the plague was in the soil and the water?" Chato interrupted.

"Ah, it is, in a form of magic from the magic stones themselves, where dragons draw on their power. Magic is not as simple as we would think it is. Come inside," she said. Crimson and Chato moved inside the den. Azuran's head moved into view, and his blue eyes peered in. Crimson could see a dull glow from one of the stones along the wall; Galena hadn't moved them. It seemed she hadn't needed to use them either. The roots from the ceiling had grown longer, reaching almost to the reddish-colored soil on the bottom of the den.

"You may take that one," Galena said to the small glowing stone across the room. "As I told you before, the magic is almost gone."

"Before we go," Chato said, "what do you know about the magic under the lake?"

"How do you come to know of this power?"

"Does it matter?" Azuran said.

"I know whatever is there should not be disturbed," Galena said.

"But what is it? Do you know?" Chato asked.

"I have my suspicions but nothing certain. You need to leave the matter alone."

"But Azuran wants us to help him find it," Crimson said.

"Does he?" Galena said. "Did you go in search of it, Crimson?"

"I did, but I couldn't reach it. I felt it."

Galena twitched her ears. "Leave it where it is; you must for all of our sakes."

She moved toward the den entrance.

"How would a dragon come to know of this power?" she asked.

Azuran's eyes narrowed.

"A dragon with tusks has a lot of mysteries. Do you care to share?"

"Do you know of the power or not?" Azuran growled.

Galena did not seem afraid of him in the least. She placed her paw on Azuran's scaled snout. A spark flashed between her paw and his nose. "I know who you are, and I know what you want. You cannot have it. It is dark magic that must never be disturbed."

Azuran's eyes opened wide. They fixated in terror on something that only he could see. A high-pitched scream came from his mouth, and then his eyes closed. He opened them a moment later. "What did you do?" he cried. His blue eyes flashed with anger, and he moved his head threateningly toward Galena.

Crimson moved between them. "No, Azuran."

"I showed you the future. There is only death under the lake. Leave it where it is."

Chato stood still, stunned by what had happened.

"How?" Crimson said.

"Magi receive messages from the great Magi of

the past. Sometimes it is dreams, sometimes visions. Knowledge is passed from Magi to Magi."

"Amber told me that, but I didn't know you could share it."

"You have much to learn."

Azuran's head moved out of view as he backed away. He was clearly unsettled by what he had seen.

"Azuran knows now what the serpent leader wants and what it will cost. He has his answer," Galena said. "Go and heal your dragon, Crimson."

Chato picked up the stone in his mouth and moved out of the den with Crimson.

"Thank you, Galena," Crimson said. *What power does Galena have? What powers do Magi have? She didn't even use a stone.* There was so much more she wanted to ask, but now was not the time. She had to get back to her dragon.

Azuran followed the Norterridane out of the thorns and lifted them once again into the darkening sky.

"Take us to the Underground," Crimson said, wondering what the Magi had shown him.

Azuran did not speak, lost in this own thoughts.

CHAPTER 17

AZURAN carried Crimson and Chato over the trees toward the Underground City. He set the pair down a few feet from the dense shrubs that hid the western entrance. Crimson had used this entrance many times going to and from her home in the redwood forest.

The guards at the entrance did not question their hurried return. Explorers were well known and often traveled in and out of the city in great haste. Crimson had gained quite a bit of fame herself from the serpent battle, and though she was rarely in the city, everyone knew her by her unique fur color. They reached the Magi den and stepped in. Amber leaned over Covelli. Crimson's heart stopped.

Chato dropped the stone. "Amber?"

"We will not be needing it," she replied, and moved out of the way, wagging her tail. Covelli's eyes were open and she was breathing fine, taking big breaths of air.

Crimson rejoiced, looking around the Magi cave that had been turned into a damp environment. Water dripped off Covelli's scales when she sat up in the makeshift puddle in the den.

"That is good news," Chato said. "I will take this stone and place it with the others. We may need its magic for times to come."

He turned to Crimson. "I am glad your dragon is OK."

Crimson rubbed shoulders with him. He lifted the magic stone; then he moved through a tunnel at the back of the den.

"How?" Crimson said as she walked through the mud on the den floor.

"Torbern's pack found a magic stone near the cliffs, in a river flowing out of the lake. It was small but had enough magic."

"So, she will be all right?"

"She will live, but her scales will never harden, and she has insufficient dragon magic left. I cannot say what that will mean for her as she matures."

Crimson did not know what to say. Covelli would

live; that was all that mattered. The weight lifted from her shoulders.

"Crimson," a familiar voice called from the den entrance. She turned to see Beryl in the entryway. "You are needed in the Elders' cave. Amber will watch Covelli a bit longer."

Amber bowed her head.

"No cave lizards came?"

"The Magi den is far from the outer tunnels, but we were lucky none tried to break through."

Crimson gave Covelli an affectionate lick on the top of her head and darted off after Beryl.

IN THE ELDERS' cave, Ferruginous sat listening to Chato explain what had happened with Galena. Ferruginous appeared to be in deep thought. Other Elders sat in the cave as well.

"The warriors had much to tell," he said calmly. "And it seems Azuran has helped us, but we cannot be sure of his intentions. We cannot have a dragon as an enemy. What do you think he wants?"

"Besides the magic, I'm not sure." Crimson quivered slightly, unnerved by the intense stare the Elder gave her.

"I think he wants the magic for himself," Chato said. "Something about the way he wouldn't talk about it in the cave."

"He could be craving magic now that he is turning into a serpent," Beryl said.

Murmurs of affirmation erupted in the cave.

"Do you know what the magic is?" Crimson said.

"No, but we sent Lazuli to the cave-dweller ruins where you saw the hieroglyphs that possibly could tell us more about Jasper. Another glyph said that dragons can choose to share their power, or share it without even realizing it. That is why adult dragons can absorb their powers." Ferruginous paused as the room filled with chatter. He waited for the room to become quiet again before continuing. "It seems that Midnight was able to temporarily use Chalcedony's power because she let him, so this also means …"

"That Azuran is letting the serpent share his power," Crimson said in disbelief. "He was asking how to undo the bond. Is there a way?"

Voices filled the room again.

"Does that mean that a dragon is evil?" a Norterridane asked.

"It can't be possible."

"I always said something was off with those Obsidians."

Crimson let her button ears fall and tried to drown out their opinions of what was happening.

"Do you think it's true?" Crimson asked, turning toward Beryl. "Could Azuran have become evil?"

"I don't know," Beryl said. "We know very little about how dragons share power, except with us."

"Does this mean that perhaps the dragons can start protecting their own young now?" a keeper asked.

"I think not," the wise old Ferruginous said. "The younger the dragon, the less control of their power they have. I believe they share their power almost unconsciously, as an instinct for survival, and mature dragons take the power and keep it. I do not think this is conscious either. But when dragons are aware of sharing their power, they can take it back. When the dragons mature, they can feel as if part of their power is missing. When their scales harden, they feel for the power they are missing and take it back. That seems to be why the Norterridane keepers lose their power when their dragon matures and no longer needs protecting. This is also how the plague was spread. Crimson must not use her Magi powers."

Many sounds of agreement could be heard around the room.

"It seems to make sense."

"They are pretty helpless so young, and when they no longer need us, we don't need the power."

"So what does this mean for dragon keepers?" one Elder asked. "Does that change our ways of keeping?"

"We have a lot to think about if we continue to keep dragons," Labrad said. "I think we just have to be aware of how the serpents are able to get powers, and teach the young dragons that they are sharing their power. Perhaps they can become more aware of how to share and use their powers. This new knowledge tells us why the serpents are so interested in young dragons. They must have figured it out before us."

"No," Ferruginous said. "If dragons could choose not to share their power, the dragons would never have had to send them to Genorrdia. It seems that dragon powers present themselves differently with different creatures, just as it is different with you."

"We must find a new way of training and protecting dragons. Even though only one serpent seems to be able to penetrate the magic shield, we must be vigilant in training."

"What will we do?" a small sable Norterridane asked.

"We must work with the warriors, dragon keepers,

and healers to find a new way. Soon the dragons will leave the city to be safer in secret. This too will keep the Underground safe. This new threat of dragons and serpents is like no other that we have ever seen. Beryl will work closely with the healers and scribes to find new ways to keep us safer from the serpents. We still have our shields, and rebuilding goes well."

"So why am I here?" Crimson said.

"We need you to convince Azuran to give up his quest for magic and return to Alannador. The dragons can find out how the serpents have shared his power. Be careful not to divulge any information that may be useful to the serpents. The serpents may show kindness when it suits them, but they are an evil race."

"What if I cannot convince him?"

"Then the dragons will have to kill him."

"We can't."

"Jet is searching for Azuran, and Carnelian, the second scout, has gone to Alannador to Hornblende. If Azuran does not return, they have orders to find and kill him."

A few weeks before, Ferruginous granted Beryl permission to send a pack of warriors with Lazuli to investigate the caves in hopes of finding out more information on this mysterious magic under the lake. The pack set off at dawn toward the eastern Black Mountains and the Sapphire River, a journey that would take weeks to reach the caves that Crimson and Chalcedony had made their home two winters ago. But Lazuli was hopeful that she would find the answers she was looking for.

Lazuli's tail twitched. She ran with the pack toward untranslated hieroglyphs. She could hardly contain her excitement. The symbols in the caves possibly held more information that linked the history of dragons, serpents, and Norterridane, and revealed what secret Jasper had been hiding. Whatever it was, it seemed that it was important for dragon-kind and Norterridane to find out. While Ferruginous believed it would be inconsequential when it came to the serpent–dragon war, there was no harm in learning more about the past.

The journey to the ruins was long and difficult. The pack traveled through the northern redwood forest and then along the coast for weeks. The creatures in the ocean provided decent meals. But the pace at which the Norterridane traveled was brutal. Lazuli's paws hurt, and her legs slowed. But it was urgent that they find the answers to the archives before the serpents found a way to get whatever it was out of lake. When they arrived at the pine forest, it was just as Crimson had described, including the strange musky scent in the air.

"We're close," Lazuli said. The pack sniffed around and followed the scent.

"This is different than I remember," Torbern said. "Nothing but the smell of this forest seems familiar."

"How can that be?"

"It just seems different. I am sure we will pick up the trail soon."

Lazuli followed Torbern, the chosen pack leader and alpha for the mission, through the forest. The forest floor changed from dark humus to some light sandy rocks. Lazuli stepped lightly and sniffed the rocks. *Shale?* A little farther ahead, solid rock and the tree line thinned. A vast landscape of trees grew in the distance. Lazuli crept up to the edge of a rocky drop-off.

"Why is the smell so strong, if we cannot see the caves?"

"I think we are above them. Didn't Crimson say that they were built into some sort of cliff?"

Torbern sniffed. "Yes, I remember they were. We are going to have to follow the cliff and find a way down to the caves."

A warning bark from one of the pack grabbed their attention. In the distance, two creatures flew toward the cliff.

"Serpents," Torbern growled. "We have to hide in the forest. They won't be able to smell us with the cave-dweller scent so pungent here, but they can see us. Let's go."

Lazuli and the pack moved into the forest, hiding in the brush and small ferns.

Large feet hurried through the forest. Strange voices resonated through the trees. Lazuli crouched down under a fern, pressing her belly against the ground. Her heart beat faster than ever before. Being a scribe, she had not been in the serpent battle and had never seen one of the creatures up close. Its large bat-like wings brushed against the trees, knocking down pine needles and cracking branches. A large clawed foot stepped near the fern. Lazuli tensed, and then fur brushed up against her side. She turned to see Torbern gesturing for her to follow. Slowly, one paw at a time, she made her way to him. Lazuli moved from under the fern. A deer jumped out of its hiding place and sprinted away. The serpent followed.

Lazuli let out a deep breath. "That was close," she whispered.

"Imagine fighting them," Torbern whispered back. "Come on, Gypsum found the path." A fern covered his muzzle, making him look whole again. Lazuli didn't mind the scar though. It showed that he had been in battle, a brave and capable leader. The mark of a true warrior.

Lazuli and the pack ran down the sloping hill that would lead to the caves. They stayed alert and moved swiftly though the forest. The best chance of staying undetected was to find the caves and keep their scent masked.

The path opened abruptly, and Lazuli gazed upon a magnificent structure, with strange rocks piled to make the squared opening to many large caves. Lazuli dashed ahead, heart pounding and energy renewed. She had to know what mysteries lay inside.

She jumped through an opening in the nearest cave. She sniffed the floor and the walls. Many strange and unfamiliar scents entered her nose. *Was Crimson here in this cave?* No smells of dragons or Norterridane, other than the pack that had come with Lazuli. Strange scents along the walls, the floor, and among the burnt wood strewn about. A musty scent clung to everything and hung in the air. The serpents would not smell them here.

Hieroglyphs showed many things from the past, and Lazuli delighted in the information. *Many hundreds of years ago, the cave-dwellers lived on Genorrdia, and their past was written here, waiting to be deciphered.*

The pack searched the caves until darkness fell upon the land. Torbern could not recall where Crimson had shown him the pictures of Genorrdia, nor the pictures of the white Norterridane. Torbern let the pack rest, checking on each one before sprawling out on the cave floor.

In the morning, they found a path that led down to another level of caves, and these seemed more familiar to Torbern.

The sun shone high when they found the cave

with the white Norterridane. The symbol showed fire surrounding Jasper.

"Just as Crimson said. Why do you think she is surrounded by fire?"

"She is surrounded, but look. She created it, or it looks like she is changing the fire into a stone."

Lazuli examined the image of the Norterridane. One symbol meant "capture," and a jagged, curved symbol meant "magic."

"Torbern, most of these symbols were made by cave-dwellers, but some were made later by someone else, and not Jasper."

"How do you know?"

"The strokes of the symbols are different. Look how the older symbols are carefully drawn."

Torbern nodded.

"These ones seem sloppy and hurried."

"Maybe they had to leave in a hurry," he suggested.

"Or it wasn't a scribe who wrote it. I don't think it was a dragon , nor a cave-dweller either. I think a Norterridane wrote this."

"What do the symbols mean?" Torbern asked.

"It says that Jasper took the power and hid it away, then disappeared. It seems like someone was telling the story of her last dragon-keeping deed, before she disappeared."

"Who told the story? I mean, who made these symbols?" Torbern asked.

"There is no way to know for sure."

"Torbern, over here," a warrior called from another section of the cave wall.

Lazuli followed Torbern to where the warrior stood. Many more symbols had been etched into the cave walls. It seemed like a jumbled mess of ancient symbols mixed with more modern ones, and cave-dweller symbols mixed with Norterridane. Some were hard to make out. "It looks like we are going to have to search every cave and decider the symbols. The answer is here somewhere; we just have to find it."

"I'll send the pack to hunt. There aren't any rivers nearby and we need to eat."

The symbols were like the ones in the Elders' cave, new and old mixed together. Lazuli looked for dragon symbols. If she couldn't decode them, she would have to have the Magi transfer them, but they would have to find more magic stones, and the explorer had not sensed any nearby.

"There doesn't seem to be anything like you described," Torbern said. "The pack has searched everywhere."

"Wait … The last hieroglyphs were hidden. There has to be a clue for something hidden. Look for this symbol," she said, scratching a symbol into the dirt-covered floor. The pack spread out to look.

Someone wanted me to find these messages, I just know it.

"Over here," Torbern called.

There it was, the same symbol that had been near the crack in the Elders' cave.

Lazuli scratched the wall. It was solid, but not stone. More like mud that had hardened and then had been carved into. She carefully scratched away the outer layer. Sure enough, solid stone lay under it, and on it, dragon symbols.

She placed her paw on the symbols. Her paw pads felt the cold. A cold that seeped into her body. She froze. Her breaths came fast and time seemed to stop. As she stared at the next symbols, a vision entered her mind.

Lazuli looked down at her paws. Her fur was white, and she stood near a magic stone larger than her paw. The air was thick and heavy. It took a moment to realize she was underwater. The magic stone glowed brightly, and looking past it, she only saw endless gray stone. Her mouth breathed in water filtered through gills, and she trembled. She picked up the stone in her mouth. Magic surrounded her, swirling in a rainbow of color. The stone beside her became transparent. She stepped into darkness.

Torbern's paw touched her, drawing her from the vision. She shuddered.

"What is it?"

"The hieroglyphs tell of Jasper. There must have been magic in these hieroglyphs, like runes. I saw her last moments. I could feel her last moments. She took the stone into the lake, deep in the lake, with her magic. She buried herself with the stone."

"What? That doesn't make sense. Why would she go through all that trouble to hide a magic stone?"

"It wasn't just a magic stone, and she didn't just hide it. She sacrificed herself to keep it safe."

"What's in it?"

"It's dark magic, pulled from the cave-dwellers and dragons. We knew she stopped the plague from spreading, but we didn't know how. That stone cannot come out of the lake. We have to warn the Elders."

"How do you know that?"

"I didn't just see her, I was there. I felt what she felt. I felt her fear and determination. She wanted this magic to be hidden forever."

"If it was meant to be hidden, how are we discovering it now?"

"Something must have uncovered it. Maybe it is not completely buried in the stone anymore."

"Erosion?"

"Possibly, but I am thinking that Jasper had magic like Crimson. When Crimson called all of the dragon magic, she may have called upon the stone as well."

"Crimson uncovered it? Then we must bury it again. How can we do that?"

"Crimson has to be trained like Jasper so she can find out how to bury it."

"But Jasper is gone. She sacrificed herself. Crimson can't do that."

"The Elders will have to decide what to do. We must return to the Underground.

CRIMSON and Covelli rested by Crystal Lake. The sun was high in the sky, and not a cloud in sight. Covelli's scales shone brilliant turquoise in the light. Crimson giggled. For a dragon who needed water, she sure liked to dry her scales out in the sun. Covelli would go back and forth from the water to the sand, alternating from the wet to the dry. She was so very different from the Obsidian hatchling, who enjoyed water but preferred to explore on land.

Beryl's scent came through the reeds with the breeze, along with the rustling sound of his steps on the plant leaves.

"Lazuli has returned," he said.

Crimson knew that for Beryl to come, it must be important.

"What did she find out?"

"Lazuli confirmed what Galena said about the power. It is dark magic. The cave-dwellers created the magic that is under the lake, and Jasper hid it there. The Elders believe that the magic is the plague, or at least whatever magic the cave-dweller used to start the plague. The spores that spread the plague were in the water, soil, and air in Alannador. It even locked itself within the bodies of dragons. Jasper stopped it from spreading, and the Elders believe she did it by sacrificing herself. She put the magic in the stone, and she sealed herself in a tomb."

"Why would Jasper bring a stone with horrible dark magic here?" Crimson said, walking with Beryl and Covelli into the water. Covelli swam in the shallow water at the lake's edge. She played with snails, knocking them off plants and rocks and watching them sink to the bottom.

"Lazuli said she had to take it as far away from the cave-dwellers as possible. She didn't think they would look here on Genorrdia, and it seems like she was right," Beryl said.

"How can we be sure she is down there with it?"

"Because Lazuli saw and felt the last moments of her life."

"That is powerful magic," Crimson said. "What does it all mean?"

"Ferruginous believes that the stone is taking the magic from the other magic stones. It is siphoning the power. The explorers sensed it."

Beryl looked down a moment at the ground. He seemed to be searching for the right words.

"Something awakened the power of the stone … and we believe it was you."

"What? How is that possible?"

"The Elders are not sure how, but, yes, they believe so. Perhaps when you called on so much dragon power, you awakened the stone. They also believe that when you connected with the magic in the stone while using Covelli's power, you gave her the plague. They are discussing ways to stop the magic from growing. A key might be in Alannador."

Crimson's head was spinning. She didn't know enough about her magic to trust herself with it now. If she had really caused the plague in Covelli, and awakened an evil magic-stealing power, then she wasn't a protector, she was a danger to everyone.

"And he wants me to see if I can put it back to sleep?" Crimson said, putting the pieces together.

"In a manner of speaking, yes. Amber will be here shortly to continue your training, but you may have to learn from dragons. There is talk of you going to Alannador once Covelli flies."

"Why there?"

"The death dragon can communicate with the ancestors, and she can teach you how to channel the dragon magic. Carnelian believes that you will need a lot of power to reseal the stone.

Covelli brought a mouthful of snails out of the lake and dropped them off in the den, then she slashed in the lake to collect more.

"I have some other bad news," Beryl said.

Crimson perked up her ears. Her head ached trying to understand all that he had just said, and there was more?

He stood tall and proud, like he always did as alpha warrior, but something in his demeanor seemed caring and even a little worried.

"I know you have a lot on your mind, but I have to tell you Bowen has disappeared. He was supposed to return weeks ago, and search parties found no sign of him or Olivine."

"Does Tourmaline know?" Crimson asked, her mind still racing, trying to grasp everything about a magical plague-filled stone, and now what her mother must be feeling.

"Yes, she does. I thought I should be the one to tell you," Beryl said.

"Is she OK?"

"As can be expected. Not knowing is the hardest part."

"And what am I supposed to do with that information? It's not like I can fly off looking for him."

"Watch your tone, Crimson. Don't do anything. Let the alphas handle this. If your father is alive … they will find him."

The slight pause in his voice made Crimson wonder if he believed that.

"You have to concentrate on the threat at hand. Focus on learning to be a Magi. You may be the only one who can keep the dark magic at bay."

Crimson thanked Beryl for the news. He had to be the one to tell her. She tried not to think of her father or Azuran. It was nearly impossible. All she could do now was wait for Amber.

NATURE SEEMED to mirror Crimson's sullen mood. Horizontal lines of rain fell pitter-pattering on the ground, splashing up slightly as each droplet impacted, as if deliberately trying to cause a disruption to the peaceful land below. Then the crack of thunder rang out round the valley. Crimson lay her chin down on her front paws, relaxed her ears, and tried to quiet the storm. It was no use. The storm grew louder, and thunder boomed. Water poured down into the den.

Covelli, however, was in high spirits. She splashed around in the rain, delighting in it as if she did not spend most of her life in water. It was the season of rain; soon the leaves would fall, and after that, snow. Covelli would mature before that. Sea dragons did not take very long to mature.

"Amber may not come in this storm. Shall we swim?"

Covelli followed Crimson into the lake. After several feet, the splashing of raindrops was far above them. Crimson looked off toward the crevasse. It seemed like the best place to hide a magic stone. She made sure they swam far from it. She didn't want to risk calling on the dragon plague again.

"I bet your mother would have taken you to explore in the ocean," Crimson said to Covelli.

Covelli fluttered her wings.

"Let's race."

Covelli dashed off through the water at a tremendous speed, and Crimson had to paddle fast to keep up. She swam through the lake, letting go of everything that had happened. Crimson surfaced and splashed water on Covelli. The small dragon swung her tail, and a small swirling wave glided toward Crimson. They played for hours, and when they were finally exhausted, the pair walked sluggishly toward the den. Amber awaited their return.

"Fun swim?"

"Exactly what I needed," Crimson said, and Covelli fluttered her wings. She placed them on her side, holding them off the ground.

"She is getting stronger," Amber said. "Are you ready for your next lesson?"

"Sure," Crimson said. "I wonder how the serpents knew about it. The power, I mean."

"They have Magi, but they don't call them that. They call them stone-readers; they find magic. But most serpents are drawn to magic anyway."

"So that is how Azuran knows about it."

"Have you heard from him?" Amber said.

"Not since he brought us home from Galena's den."

"All right, the bad news. I was going to show you how to change stone properties, but we are running so low on magic stones that we don't want to use them needlessly. If the serpent threat becomes imminent, then we will use them. Until then, we just have to use regular stones and learn what you would do."

"How are we going to get more magic stones?"

"The dragons may be able to help if they bring some from the forest or the mountains. Some suggest they bring some from Alannador. Until then we have to wait."

CHAPTER 20

THE vision of the future would not leave his mind. Azuran stood on the Black Mountains. Thousands of bodies, both dragon and serpent, littered the ground. A serpent moved toward him, deep lacerations upon his face. His red eyes scared and pleading. Green goo poured out of his nostrils and he staggered for breath. A plague. A plague that killed serpents.

Could this really be the future that Galena had seen? What did that Magi know, anyway? Perhaps it was a trick that she showed him to keep him from the magic. Yes, maybe that was it. It had to be. But in his core, he knew he had seen the truth.

Azuran's Obsidian claws sank deep into the cliffside. He moved carefully, hiding in the dark and making sure he was undetected. He wanted to speak with Onixian before he told Malachite what he had seen. They would probably send him back anyway. Why would they believe him?

He arrived at the serpent caves and searched for Onixian; he was nowhere to be found. Azuran moved up to one of the serpents working on perfecting his sleeping space. The serpent was stretching out deer fur to lie on.

"Have you seen Onixian?" he asked.

The serpent glared at him but answered anyway. "At the meeting place. Probably will be back soon, dragon."

Azuran flew toward the rock cliff that Malachite had chosen to hold private meetings with his most trusted advisors. The moon cast a soft glow, and the dark cliff stood out among the snow-covered peaks. Ocean waves splashed in the distance.

Azuran stood at the base of the cliff on the snow-covered beach. The cliff rose more than one thousand feet into the sky. It looked as if one of the spiraled ice peaks had been sliced in half by a dragon claw, and the top chopped off. It was the only real cliff in this snowy mountain region. Anything flying up would be detected easily, and so climbing was his only choice. The Schorl did not have claws that could cut into stone, so the meeting place for the king and his advisors was well hidden. Normally, Azuran would not have cared about what the serpents talked about, but Galena had put thoughts in his mind. Worrisome thoughts about Malachite's hunger for power, about his own hunger for power.

Claws stabbed into the stone and he began his ascent. The climb was surprisingly easy for him, and he neared the top sooner than expected. Though he knew his claws could break stone, he was often amazed by his own strength. He removed his right claws from the stone and moved his arm up, stabbing into the stone higher up, then the left. He stuck his tongue over the cliff edge, tasting the air. The serpents were nearby but not close to the edge. He peeked his head up over the edge. He held still. The wind blew steadily here on the mountain peak, but in spite of the wind, Azuran could make out Malachite's rough voice. Tilting his head slightly to the right, he heard the voice more clearly.

"Is it really possible that Azuran is turning into a serpent?" Fairburn said.

"Perhaps the magic moves both ways," Onixian said.

"If this is true, we could turn many young dragons into half-serpents. We could build an army."

"We just have to get dragon eggs. They will have no tie to their kind."

Azuran raised his head to listen closer.

"It doesn't matter. He is still a dragon, and our enemy," Malachite argued, his words piercing Azuran's heart much more than he would ever admit.

"He has shown loyalty," Onixian said, and Azuran could see him moving closer to the serpent king in defiance. "He is off making friends with those vile and weak creatures because you asked him to. Give him more time. This is a new era; we have to embrace it."

"That is the problem: if we keep dragons instead of killing them, they must be one hundred percent loyal. No possibility of turning. Azuran may be useful now, but how long do you really expect him to stay? How long until he decides he is with the dragons and kills us all?"

Onixian roared in protest but did not deny Malachite's words.

"We went about it all wrong in our greed to take our land back. We will take the power from this land and bide our time to become more powerful. We will find out what is stripping the magic from the stones. We will get the power in the lake, even if I have to bring all the serpents from Calimdural and drain the entire thing."

Fairburn and Onixian nodded in agreement.

"We will take over this continent."

Malachite turned to Onixian. "You have to be ready. When we find this powerful magic and the dragon war is over … If Azuran betrays us, we have to kill him."

Onixian did not utter a word in protest, which hurt Azuran far more than any words Malachite could have said. Azuran released his grip and let himself fall, opening his wings to glide away only when he was sure he was out of earshot. That was the vision. Malachite bringing the serpents to Genorrdia, and a plague. He could almost feel the sickness of it in his body. The vision of so many dying would not leave his mind. He let the wind carry him down to the hard ground of the Black Mountains. He knew serpents were cruel, but he thought he had gained some sort of place amongst their kind, and for a moment, he hated Onixian for not just killing him as a hatchling. He hated craving magic. His limbs grew heavy. He slumped on the icy surface and he sat in the darkness underneath the cliff. He turned and stabbed his tusks into the stone wall. Bits of stone fell to the ground. His chest heaved. Anger rose inside him.

With a heavy heart, he returned to his lair on the ice peak.

Azuran lay down and closed his eyes. Not for the first time in his life, he heard a pleasant melody. It seemed farther away now than the first time he had heard it, but it was the same song. It called for him to leave Genorrdia and fly west. He lifted his head, feeling the melody call to him, but the visions Galena had put in his mind flooded in. He had to find out what that power was, and he knew now that Malachite couldn't have it. He would stay, and he would kill Malachite before he could kill him. He could save them all.

A ROAR SHATTERED THE SILENCE. Azuran ran out from his cave. Two large black dragons battled in the stone amongst the serpents. Their words in dragon tongue shouted in his mind.

"I've got this one."

"Move back!" A tail slashed and slammed into a serpent, sending him flying backward. The large Obsidian male had spines down his back similar to Azuran's. The smaller female dragon, who had smooth scales and fierce blue eyes, stalked the serpents as they moved, trying to attack but also fearing the Obsidian claws. A serpent moved too close, and a claw sliced down its shoulder to its elbow. Blood poured onto the snow.

"They know they can't win. Why are they fighting?" The large Obsidian's voice came into this mind.

"They are waiting for something."

"Malachite," Azuran replied in dragon tongue, effortlessly, like he had spoken with Covelli.

"Azuran, we came to find you. Jet and I have come to take you to Alannador," the female said.

"Carnelian, look out!"

Andalus jumped off of an ice pillar, attempting to land on the dragon's back. She moved in time, but red-tipped tusks sliced a gash across her side. She rolled out of the way, eyes blazing.

"You're not invincible after all," Andalus said in the common tongue.

Carnelian responded with a breath of hot blue fire. Andalus stepped back; the fire had hurt him, but not nearly enough.

"You have gained quite a lot of power," Carnelian said. "But will it be enough? Again flames sprouted from her mouth and blasted into Andalus. Jet joined her, searing several serpents. The serpents began to back away.

Malachite jumped down from the pillar and landed in the fray. He swung his massive tail, slamming Carnelian in the face. She brushed it off as if nothing had hit her. Jet attacked, slicing at Malachite, making deep wounds in his magic-enhanced scales, but Jet was avoiding the tusks, and a cruel sardonyx-covered claw slashed across his face. Scales fell to the ground, and blood covered Jet's face.

"Attack!" Malachite commanded, and the serpents rushed in. They seemed unconcerned with their own lives and mercilessly attacked the dragons. Their claws slid off scales, but still they attacked. One by one the serpents were wounded, but they kept attacking, trying to keep the attention away from the claws and tusks that could kill them.

Andalus stabbed his tusks through Carnelian's leg. She blew fire and killed several serpents. Then came a blood-curdling scream; Malachite's tusks stabbed through Jet's neck. Then Malachite stuck his tusks though the dragon's heart, absorbing the Obsidian magic as Jet died. "Why are you standing there?" Carnelian's pained cry came into Azuran's mind. She beat her wings, but a serpent jumped on top of one, pinning her down. She blasted him with fire. There were too many serpents to fly away. "Help me!"

Fire burned more serpents. Many were dead on the ground, either from fire or calculated hits with Obsidian claws.

"Azuran, I am your mother."

And inside his mind, he saw her memory, clear as day, covering two gray Obsidian eggs. He heard her voice through his eggshell. A feeling of love and warmth flowed through him.

He leapt from the ground. Feeling the fire turn in his stomach, he sprayed the serpents holding her down with bright blue fire. His tail whipped and smashed into Andalus's face, stunning him. The moment of surprise was just enough. Carnelian lifted her wings and flew into the sky. Azuran followed, looking back to see Malachite's evil glare as he fled. The serpents could not match their speed in the air, and those that gave chase quickly gave up.

Azuran followed her as best he could, but he did not have as much endurance flying. "Wait!" he called.

Carnelian glided down to a wooded area and landed within the trees. Her side and leg bled heavily. She turned and breathed a smoke-filled fire along her scales.

"There, that will stop the bleeding for now."

Azuran could feel the weight of her gaze upon him, and for the first time, he felt ashamed. He moved his wing to cover his tusks.

"Do not hide, my son."

"You don't hate me? I have betrayed our kind. I have … I didn't—"

Carnelian slowly moved her leg, wincing at the pain. "I forgot what it was like to be injured. It's been so long."

She curled her tail over her wound. "Fire only heals so much."

"Why didn't you bring sardonyx? You could have killed all of them."

"There is not much left, I'm afraid. The war may turn in favor of the serpents soon," Carnelian said, "Enough of war. I want to know about you, my son, and I want to tell you of all the wonders that await you on Alannador."

Azuran sighed. He felt so close to Carnelian, and they talked well into the darkness. But he couldn't help feeling he had abandoned Onixian.

CHAPTER 21

CRIMSON tried to push all the negative thoughts in her mind away. Lazuli's return had shaken her for some time. She worried about her mother, her father, and Azuran, whom she had not seen since he dropped her and Chato off at the Underground City. And she worried about the magic stone in the lake that seemed to be absorbing magic from other stones. If she hadn't become a dragon keeper, she wouldn't have had to worry about any of it. She could have stayed in ignorant bliss, hearing tales of how amazing and honorable being a dragon keeper was.

A surprise came that day when Midnight came to visit, or check on her as per Beryl's orders. He was walking quite well, even with his wounded shoulder.

"You seem much better," Crimson commented as he approached. "So glad to see you."

"Yeah. Amber says I am ready to rejoin the warriors. I will be able to patrol soon, and later I will be able to keep another dragon. Though I want to wait on that a bit longer."

Crimson wagged her tail and gazed fondly on Midnight. "I don't need you to check on me," she said, "but I'm glad you came."

Midnight hushed her and crouched to the ground. "A dragon approaches."

A black shape grew larger and larger in the sky. Azuran had returned. Covelli jumped up and down, and despite Crimson's caution, she moved closer to Azuran.

"I won't hurt you," he said.

"You have grown," Midnight said, staying cautious of the dragon. He stood near the den, most likely to call upon a magical shield if needed.

"Midnight, you would be proud of the fierce dragon I have become," Azuran said.

"Dragons kill to protect, not for power," Midnight said calmly.

"I came to get your help, as you agreed," Azuran said to Crimson.

"We can't help you. The Elders said that the magic is the dragon plague and other dark magic."

Azuran moved back, his head low. "I have seen a future where dragons and serpents are dead by the thousands. The serpents plan to get the magic out. They want me to help them."

"How?" Crimson asked.

"They believe that draining the lake is the way to the magic. They will destroy the city if they have to."

"Why are you telling me this?"

Azuran stood quiet. Crimson still wondered where his loyalty lay. But she knew that if the serpents retrieved the dark magic, then the whole world would be in danger, not just Genorrdia.

"Because they cannot have the power, and we are no longer allies. The dragons came to find me, and Jet paid for that mistake with his life."

"What happened?"

Azuran summed up what had happened.

"You met your mother? Where is she now?"

"She was wounded and has stayed in the forest near the mountains.

"Is she going to be OK?" Crimson said.

"I think so."

"If you agree that the serpents can't have the magic, what are you doing here?" Midnight said.

"I need the power to kill Malachite. The only way to end his quest for magic, and for blood, is to kill him."

"You don't need more power to kill him; you're an Obsidian," Crimson said. "Why not just kill him?"

"I am not sure I can. He has gained so much power. He took it from Jet. I fear I will not have enough. He has killed two Obsidian dragons. I am not invincible as you say Obsidian should be. Sharing my power has made me weak. I saw how he killed Jet. If I do not become stronger, I will share the same fate."

"The magic under the lake is trapped in solid stone. There is no way to get it, and even if I could get it, I don't think you can harness the power."

"Serpents can absorb magic from stones."

"I still don't see how we could get it. We would need your claws and you cannot breathe underwater."

Azuran crouched down, hiding his body in the reeds. A green dragon flew over the hills toward the redwood forest.

"An earth dragon," he breathed, staring in awe at her scales glittering in the sun. It was seen only for a second, then vanished in the sky. As if she forgot to camouflage herself. "What is she doing here?"

"She came to lay eggs," Midnight said, more to himself than to the two sitting near him.

"Dragons share power, right?" Azuran said.

"You can't use dragon power to fight Malachite," Midnight said.

"Why not?" Azuran's eyes flashed an interrogative look. "Crimson used it to fight the serpents."

"That's different. I was protecting—"

"They are my kind, not yours!" Azuran roared.

"A hatchling needs protection; that is why they share magic. It's not magic for your own personal gain," Midnight said. "Crimson, you cannot let him take it."

"What would your mother say?" Crimson said, trying to appeal to another side of him. "Surely Carnelian would object."

"I'm certain she wants the serpent who killed Jet dead."

"The Elders must know of this. Keep an eye on him, Crimson," Midnight said, and dove into the water.

"You won't make it to the Elders before I reach the egg," Azuran said confidently.

He spread his wings, and Crimson called upon his power, not just to feel it and connect with him, but to stop him. Her claws glowed with white-hot flames. She felt his power and knew Azuran was right; his power was weaker now. Nowhere near the power she had felt when he had first come to see her.

"What are you doing?" Azuran growled as he stumbled over.

Covelli screeched and fled into the den.

"What are you doing? You are killing me!" Azuran howled in agony. His wings went limp and clawed at the ground.

Crimson let go of his power. "Azuran, I … I was just …"

He opened his wings with full force, knocking her back onto the sand. Her head spun and a sharp pain throbbed between her eyes. When she finally got to her feet, Azuran was gone.

CHAPTER 22

*A*ZURAN flew toward the redwood forest. The sun was setting, and he hid within the shadows of the trees, as Onixian had taught him to do when he hunted. He had no intention of killing the dragon. But he would if he had to. *The Norterridane can't stop this; only I can. Only I can prevent the future.*

He felt weak, but he believed his strength would return. *How could she do that, use her power on me again? I thought she cared about me.* Somehow that thought hurt more than it should have. *Why should I care about her? She is nothing to me.* Tears burned at his eyes. He blinked them away. He gazed into the forest and set his mind to his task. *Get the dragon egg.*

He wasn't sure how the magic-sharing would work. He could take the egg to Carnelian and she would tell him. She would understand, and they could fight Malachite together.

Azuran waited, hidden within the forest, still as the trees themselves, just as Onixian had taught him. He watched the earth dragon as she surveyed the area once more.

The earth dragon looked at the egg she had laid and covered it with a fresh pile of dirt. She spoke in dragon tongue to it. Azuran heard her. "Be safe, my darling. I await you on Alannador, big and strong. The keepers will find you soon. They will care for you as I would have."

The dragon spread her wings and flew, low in the forest for a few wingbeats, and then vanished. Azuran was thankful he did not accidentally speak in dragon tongue and alert her to his presence.

Azuran listened until the wingbeats could no longer be heard.

Azuran's hearing was not the best, but he could hear something moving. He stuck out his tongue and tasted the air. Norterridane were on the way, swiftly moving through the forest. Azuran moved out of his hiding place and dug up the freshly piled soil. Within seconds he had uncovered the egg. It was pale green with speckled dots of yellow and brown. It was much smaller than he had thought a dragon egg would be. He lifted it in his claws and flew out of the forest toward Mount Xenoti, and the forest where Carnelian had stayed. In that moment, his heart beat fast. A moment later, and he would have been discovered. It occurred to him that he was a dragon and he easily could have killed the Norterridane, but he wondered if perhaps more of them had powers like Crimson. The unknown made him cautious. After all, they protected dragons; they must be powerful.

The thumping of a heartbeat grew in his mind, louder than his own heart. His muscles tingled and his heart beat in unison with the unhatched dragon's. He knew it was the heartbeat from the egg within his claws. A rush of heat entered his body, connecting him with the unhatched dragon. The feeling was so intense that weakness overcame him, and he could no longer fly. He glided down and landed on the side of a large cliff in the shadows of Mount Xenoti.

His eyes closed. It seemed as if nothing else mattered at that moment but the heartbeat and the magic from the unhatched dragon suddenly swirling through his body. There he lay on the ground, curled in a ball with his wings folded over his body and around the egg. Listening to the heartbeat, and feeling the warmth of dragon magic, made him feel a peace he had never known.

He knew not how long he lay there with the dragon egg. He knew that she was a female. He did not know how. It must have been the dragon connection. *Do the Norterridane feel this way when they connect, or is it dragons alone who feel this way with their kind?* He sensed her magic fully at that moment. The dragon power she willingly shared. His claw began to shimmer and fade, becoming transparent and then invisible. He gasped. Onixian had told him how the earth dragons of the forest had the power of invisibility, but to feel it was unbelievable.

"I am a dragon like you, little one." A tear rolled down his cheek. Never before had he known such acceptance. It was as if the dragon loved him, with a magic beyond sight and hearing. As he brushed it away, the hard bone of his serpent tusks brushed his hand, reminding him of his quest, and tears flowed freely from his eyes.

What have I become? What did Onixian turn me into?

He gazed fondly at the small green egg. He wanted to protect the unborn dragon. He wanted to keep her safe from all the dangers of the world. At that moment, he knew why Onixian had not been able to kill him when he fell from the waterfall. He knew why he had been raised as a serpent, and he also knew he could not use the dragon to fight Malachite. The bond was too strong; there was nothing like it in the world. There had to be another way.

Onixian must have felt that connection, surely. Onixian wouldn't kill him; he knew that now. He could not let this precious dragon share her power with a serpent and be weakened as he was.

Crimson's words were wise, but he knew it would only be a matter of time before the serpents found a way to the stone, even if it meant going through the Underground, and then they would kill him. It was always about the hunger for magic.

Azuran made up his mind. Though the connection was strong, he had to return the dragon egg to the Norterridane. They would protect it. He would stop Malachite from getting the power under the lake, somehow, and the serpents could leave for Calimdural. Onixian would be safe. For though he was raised to crave power, he did not want Onixian to die for it.

Wingbeats grew near. He tasted the wind. Serpents. They must have seen him flying toward the mountain. He stood up, holding the egg in his right talons.

Malachite and Onixian landed beside him on the cliff top. Andalus, Hesson, and several other serpents landed quite a distance away, farther from the cliff's edge. Beyond the cliff, the mountain peak loomed overhead, and just beyond it, the peak of Mount Xenoti.

"We wondered where you had gone," Malachite said, and then tasted the air. A broad smile spread across his face, showing his sharp teeth. He stepped closer to Azuran. "You found an egg?"

"Yes," Azuran said reluctantly. "I also found out about the power in the mountain. I am not going to get the stone. It is a dangerous magic created by the cave-dwellers. It's the dragon plague that they corrupted. It is evil magic."

"Is that so?" Malachite said, so calmly it almost seemed as if he understood Azuran's defiance. "If that is true, we could use it to kill all the dragons, and we will rule the world."

"I have seen what it can do. It will kill all of us, not only the dragons."

"Is that why you betrayed us, helping the Obsidian dragon? Well, Azuran, did you bring the dragon egg to offer instead? So we will welcome you back?"

Azuran said nothing. He scanned the group of serpents, waiting for any movements.

Malachite laughed. "Since when do you make the decisions, dragon?" He emphasized the word *dragon,* and the nearby serpents moved closer. "You think I have not noticed your scales paling in color? How you avoid getting too close to battling serpents? Something is wrong, young dragon. Perhaps you have lived with serpents too long. Your power has faded. Give me the egg, Azuran. Give me the egg and I will allow you to live."

Is that why Malachite had talked about killing him? How long had he known his Obsidian powers had weakened? It didn't matter though. He was not going to give malachite the egg.

Azuran stood tall and defiant. "I can't do that."

"It seems you have outlived your usefulness," Malachite roared, and charged toward him.

Azuran was at a disadvantage with only one hand free. He opened his wings and hovered in the air, kicking at the king with his back legs. Malachite jumped into the air, slicing at Azuran with his six arms. The claws stung a bit, but not much. They barely scratched him. He sliced a gash into one of Malachite's arms. Blood splattered to the ground.

"So, you are stronger than I thought!" Malachite said, and came in full force, his six arms slicing.

Azuran blocked the attack with his forearms, and in that moment, he felt the most excruciating pain. A red-tipped claw stabbed into his right hand. The egg fell. Azuran swiped his left hand to catch it, and Malachite tried too, but it fell fast and hit the ground. The egg cracked open.

Azuran had to distract the king. Maybe he could repair the egg. He could only hope other serpents would not attack him too.

"Onixian, help me!" Azuran pleaded.

Onixian's eyes flashed. He looked from Azuran to Malachite, seemingly deciding what choice would give him more power.

Onixian jumped forward toward Malachite. Their heads smashed as they fought tusk against tusk, claw against claw. Azuran jumped forward, slicing his claws down Malachite's back. Small cuts appeared on the hardened scales, but again, hardly any damage was done. He had to stay away from the red claws.

Blood dripped from Onixian's glassy black scales. But he fought on.

"See what joining with a dragon has gotten you?

You should have killed him and taken his power," Malachite teased.

Azuran jumped on his back again but was shaken off and knocked to the ground.

"Oh, is that so?" Onixian said, red eyes staring back.

"Your time has come," Malachite said, stepping closer to Azuran.

"Not quite," Azuran said, a wide smile forming across his scaled mouth.

Malachite barely had time to register why the young dragon was smiling, before Onixian's large clawed feet stomped into his back. His arms grabbed Malachite furiously, and his sharp dragon-power-enhanced claws sliced into his throat, barely leaving a mark, but Onixian left no room for a counterattack. As he slashed furiously, Azuran gathered his strength to join in. Then he felt magic pulling away from him. The magic power that came from the earth dragon egg. It faded as quickly as it had come. He pulled at it with his mind. It was too late. The dragon was dead.

Tears blinded Azuran's eyes. He wiped them away, anger replacing the sudden rush of sadness when the power faded. Malachite and Onixian were in an intense battle.

Malachite thrust forward, aiming his tusks at

Onixian's heart. Onixian moved to the side, the tusks scraping against his shoulder. Malachite jumped into the air and drove his arms full force into Onixian and then smashed his head into Onixian's, knocking him backward. Then he grabbed each one of his arms, holding him in place while stabbing his tusk into Onixian's chest. Onixian screamed in pain.

Andalus and Hesson stood watching, waiting for Malachite's word to join in.

Azuran slammed his body into Malachite, breaking Onixian free. The serpents cheered for their leader. Azuran focused and slashed at Malachite's side, drawing blood. He jumped back to evade the cruel sardonyx-covered claw, but he did not jump far enough, and the claw scratched across his right leg. Blood poured freely from the wound.

"Kill him!" the serpents yelled.

Azuran fought with renewed strength, making tiny cuts along Malachite's six arms. Azuran roared as Malachite's unaltered claw sliced along his neck. Without the power from the dragon eggs, Azuran was not an invincible Obsidian. Even Malachite's black claws sent pain searing through his body. *How did I become so weak? Crimson? She must have pulled my strength from me at the lake.*

"Please help me," Azuran whispered, and called

in dragon tongue with his mind. He recalled Jet fighting and knew what he must do. Azuran snapped his braided tail, slamming it into Malachite's side. The serpent shook briefly but seemed mostly unaffected. The amount of magic he had acquired gave him unmatched strength.

Malachite launched forward at Azuran, bent on destroying him. His red claws were outstretched and swiping. Though Azuran was certain now, he was weak enough for any serpent to kill him. Azuran took advantage of the opportunity by moving his wing in front of his face and exposing it to Malachite's tusks, a calculated movement. As the red-tipped talons stuck painfully into his wing, he bit down and crunched on them. The claws ripped from the serpent's hand as Malachite pulled away, screaming in pain.

Malachite's tusks stabbed through Azuran's wing; it tore as the tusks pulled out and sliced down along the length of it. Malachite backed up and looked at his hand. He shook his head and glared at Azuran. Malachite used his other five arms to attack the dragon, trying to knock him off-balance so he could stab again.

Azuran parried the attacks; some stuck, while others missed. Just a moment longer was all he needed. Azuran crunched the claws under his molar teeth, breaking the large pieces into bits, and he swallowed them down. Pleased and grateful for the rumble of his fire stomach.

Now! he told himself.

He opened his mouth, and the hot white fire, enhanced by crystalline sardonyx, sprayed onto the serpent.

In seconds, Malachite's once proud and magic-filled body turned into ash. For a moment, an ash serpent stood, his mouth open in disbelief, and then it blew away with the wind.

Azuran turned toward the crowd of serpents. Andalus moved forward for a moment; perhaps he thought he could kill him. Azuran sucked in a breath.

The Schorl scattered from the hillside, fearful of his magic breath. When they disappeared from view, Azuran let out a roar of pain. A single tear rolled down from his eye. Why did it have to end this way? Pain poured over his body. It ached from the many claw wounds.

He picked up the broken dragon egg.

"What have I done?"

A pale green dragon lay lifeless in his hands.

He turned, wing bleeding rapidly. He dared not breathe fire to heal himself, for fear he would turn his wing to ash. He did not know how long the sardonyx would last in his system. He did not know enough about how the stones worked in dragons. He moved slowly, claws stabbing into the stone to hold his weight. A cool breeze blew by the cliffside. Azuran stumbled, weak from the loss of blood. *Imagine an Obsidian dying from blood loss. I would be the shame of dragons and serpents alike.*

He needed to reach the lake. It was his only chance of survival. A glimmer of hope.

He moved to the edge of the cliff. He feared his wing would not hold him in the air, but leapt from the cliff, holding the wounded wing as straight as possible. He glided and fell from the mountain; then he crashed into the reeds near the lake. His bones ached, and he could no longer lift his wing. The weight of the seemingly dead limb pressed down upon him. He crawled along the shore, dragging his wing with him.

"Crimson," he called, hoping that she would be near, hoping she had stayed among the reeds. He shouldn't have hurt her. She had been his friend.

But it was too late. He was going to die. Die before he even knew who to be.

Azuran turned and placed the broken egg on the ground. He breathed the hot fiery breath he had been holding in. The eggshell and dragon within turned to ashes. He lifted the ashes and let the wind carry them away. He collapsed on the ground.

"I do not know the song," he said, tears rolling from his eyes. "Go, young dragon, and find eternal life among the stars."

THEN CAME the pull on his power, so faint, yet so comforting.

"Azuran? What happened?" Crimson cried.

Azuran could no longer speak or move. His body was weak and his eyes heavy. He tried to lift his eyelids to see her one last time, but he could not.

CHAPTER 23

CRIMSON swam, heart pounding, as fast as she could toward the Underground. Covelli swam nearby and Crimson called upon her power. Her heart beat quickly as she swam, hoping she would retrieve the magic stone in time. She knew that the Elders would not approve of her bringing Covelli here again, but she couldn't let him die. She had to find Amber.

Covelli stopped at the cave entrance and buried herself under the mud.

"If a cave lizard comes, leave and get back to den. They can't swim well."

She ran up the tunnel, headed straight for the Magi den.

Midnight came out of the tunnel nearby.

"Crimson, what are you doing?"

"What are you doing here?" she shot back. Seeing his hurt look, she immediately regretted it.

"I came to see Amber about my shoulder. It's been painful now that I've been patrolling. Now answer my question."

"Azuran needs my help; he is hurt."

"He came back? What happened?"

"He is hurt, bad," Crimson said.

"The Elders don't trust him. He stole a dragon egg."

Crimson stared at Midnight; she had no words, but she pleaded with her eyes.

He looked at her as if he were going to argue, but knew it would be in vain.

"Fine. I'll go with you."

"We have to find Amber. I am hoping she still has the magic stone Galena gave me."

Midnight let out a sigh and curled up his lip. "Where is Covelli?"

"Waiting by the tunnel I had her in last time. I know it's risky. I have to find Amber. Are you coming or not?"

Midnight had no more arguments and followed Crimson as they ran down the hall to the Magi den where Covelli had recovered.

The tunnel was darker here in the Magi wing. There were fewer glow stones, but Crimson could see light radiating from the caves. A Norterridane was coming up the tunnel. Crimson tensed for a moment before she recognized her scent.

"Amber. I'm so glad you are here."

"I am meeting the pack now to leave. We are going on a search for stones. What are you doing here?"

"Azuran is hurt. I came to get you. You have to save him."

They moved quickly into the Magi den. In the back of the den, there was a wall. Amber placed her paw on the wall, and magic glowed upon it. An opening appeared. Amber went in and came out with a small, glowing white stone in her mouth. The stone that Galena had given Crimson to save Covelli.

She dropped it on the floor. "I can't help him. I have to go. You will have to use the magic in the stone."

"I'm not sure I can," Crimson said.

"Concentrate on pulling the magic from the stone and giving it to Azuran. I'm sorry, I have to go."

The wall with the opening to the magic stones resealed itself as Amber disappeared down the hall toward the warrior dens.

"If we tell the Elders, maybe they will tell her to help him."

"We protect hatchlings, not mature dragons. We are lucky Amber let us take that stone."

Crimson picked up the hard stone in her mouth.

Midnight started back the way they had come. "There is a shortcut that leads to the underwater tunnels by the lake."

Crimson moved up close to him and twitched her tail to signal she understood.

They traveled without incident to the lower caves that led to Crystal Lake, and the cool water took away some of the weight of the stress Crimson was feeling. The sun's rays showed through the water a few meters past the tunnel. Crimson, Midnight, and Covelli made their way across the lake. It seemed like an eternity had passed when they surfaced for the final time near the reeds. Midnight moved out first and sniffed the air. Crimson and Covelli joined him, smelling the dragon scent and following Midnight to where Azuran lay.

Midnight looked down at some of the ashes that had not blown away. "What happened?"

"It was a dragon egg."

"He killed it."

"Quiet," Crimson said. "You are always thinking the worst."

"And you don't think about it enough. Something happened; we told him not to take it."

"He turned it to ashes," Crimson said. "He must have seen the dragons do that when the serpent battle ended, and they grieved their dead."

"But how did he get sardonyx?"

Crimson studied Azuran, who looked different with his broken wing stretched on the ground and the two long tusks protruding from his lower jaw. The tusks had grown so fast. His eyes were closed, and he did not move. Crimson could not tell if he was breathing.

"Is he alive?"

"I'm not sure."

She placed the stone on the ground and used her claw to scratch the surface. She blocked out all other noises and concentrated on feeling the magic. It felt so far away and hard to reach.

Covelli whined beside her, touching her nose to Azuran's scales.

"I know, Covelli. I will do all I can," Crimson said. "Go into the den."

Covelli reluctantly obeyed, peeking out of the entrance with a concerned expression.

Crimson placed her paw on the stone, feeling for the magic. She looked down at her paw as the magic from the stone covered her fur with magic. She placed the paw onto Azuran's wing. She concentrated on moving the magic from her paw to his wounds. Nothing happened.

"Midnight, I don't know what to do."

Midnight moved up next to her and let her lean against him. "You can do more than anyone I have seen. If anyone can save him, it's you."

Crimson placed her paw back on Azuran and thought of the magic moving from her paw to his wing. She let go of the magic, as she would dragon magic, and slowly, sliver by sliver, the magic moved from her paw. She nearly jumped for joy when she felt it moving. It was a strange sensation; it was as if her paw was falling asleep. When at last her paw held no more magic, the tingling stopped. Azuran's skin and muscles weaved themselves together, closing the wounds. The magic stopped flowing, and blood seeped from the unclosed parts of the wound.

"There wasn't enough magic," Crimson said, and sat down in defeat.

"We have come this far; we cannot give up. He is breathing. He can be healed."

"How?" Crimson said.

"Does magic make your mind hazy? Jasperillian stops bleeding."

How could she have forgotten? She had placed the leaves on her mother's wounds the day she had found the dragon eggs and fought the cave lizard.

"I think there is some by the northern bank. Go quickly; I'll stay with Covelli."

Crimson ran through the reeds. She moved so quickly it seemed as if the reeds were smacking against her legs purposely, trying to slow her progress. When the smell of Jasperillian entered her nostrils, she smiled unconsciously. Crimson bit into the bitter-tasting leaves, breaking off a large leaf with her canine teeth. Crimson pulled off part of a larger leaf and ran back to Azuran. She dropped the leaf on the ground near Midnight. He broke the large leaf in half and walked up onto the injured wing and placed half onto the wound. He placed the other on the second wound.

"We will probably need to heal the wounds where they exit on the underwing," he said.

Midnight walked under the wing and tried to lift it with his head. It was much too heavy. The wing was three times as long as Midnight. Crimson moved to help, but it was still too large.

"What are we going to do?"

"I guess we see if we can wake him up to move his wing, or hope the magic stopped the bleeding on that side."

Crimson felt for Azuran's magic. It was faint, but it had been that way for some time. She looked at his scaled face, and the bony, spiked ridges that covered his ears.

"What if we dig under the wing?"

"That might work," Midnight replied in a solemn tone.

Midnight and Crimson dug until there was enough room for Crimson to fit under his wing. She considered the darkness created by his wing and his body. She lit her claws to see. Blood dripped from the exit wounds onto the ground.

Fire! Why didn't I think of it before? Probably because fire only closed wounds but did not repair the damage to the cells. Still, it would be a better option than Jasperillian leaves on this side of his wings. She moved her fiery paw up to the wounds. Blood dripped down into the flames and onto her paws. She watched the fire cauterize the wound. Crimson examined the wound and wondered if the broken scales that provided protective armor would regrow or remain forever gone from his body.

The dragon moved suddenly, his wing flattening

down on Crimson's body. She yelped to warn the young dragon not to crush her. He turned again, just enough for Crimson to move out of the hastily created tunnels. Weak and tired, she moved away from the dragon, into the reeds near the den, and lay down. Covelli snuggled against her.

Midnight moved beside her. "He is moving. That is a good sign."

"I couldn't let him die."

"I know," Midnight said, and placed his paw on hers. "He can tell us what happened when he wakes."

Covelli, Crimson, and Midnight lay side by side, watching the dragon breathe until Crimson's eyes grew heavy and she fell into a deep and dreamless sleep.

THE DRAGON LIFTED his head and rustled his wings. Crimson gazed at Azuran, her mind full of questions. Midnight backed up into the reeds, wary and on guard, and Covelli moved with him.

"Azuran, what happened?" Crimson said.

"I killed Malachite; he almost killed me."

Crimson breathed a sigh of relief. At least that

was one more serpent they didn't have to worry about.

"What happened with the egg, Azuran?" Midnight asked.

"The dragon is with the stars now," he replied.

"Why did you destroy the egg? Why would you kill a dragon?" Midnight said, his tone judging.

"I didn't kill her. Malachite did. He found me when I went to look for Carnelian. He knocked her from my hands. I tried to save her."

"I told you not to take the egg," Midnight said.

"Her?" Crimson said, seeing the pain on the dragon's face. The dragon grieved, and there was nothing she could say that would make this OK.

"She was an earth dragon. She …" He paused.

"Are the serpents staying here?"

"I don't know. They fled the mountain. I will find out what is to become of them."

"You shouldn't go back to them. You need to go to Alannador, Azuran. That's where you belong. Leave the rest to us," Crimson said.

"No. I have to find out where they went. I have to make sure they aren't going after the power in the lake."

"Then will you go to Alannador?"

"I am not sure I can."

"Whatever the serpents did to you, to make you grow tusks, we will find out how to fix it," Crimson said, searching for the words that would make Azuran take a chance.

"I will never be one of them." Azuran turned and looked into the sky. "I stole a dragon egg. It's my fault she died."

Crimson looked to Midnight for help. He said nothing. It seemed he was at a loss for words as well.

Crimson was a dragon keeper. He had to listen to her. If the serpents did not kill him now, she knew the dragons would later if he became a full serpent. She had to find a way to reverse it. "Chalcedony would welcome you, I know she would. You're her brother. She would forgive this mistake."

Azuran turned toward her, his piecing dark blue eyes looking into hers. "Thank you for saving my life, one day I will repay you."

"I know you'll have a place with the dragons," she said softly, placing her paw on his enormous clawed foot. Next to her he seemed a million miles away. Scales of hardest stone, that only dragon magic could break through. She felt for the magic now. That warmth that circled around her and touched her heart, which was now breaking.

The dragon closed his eyes. Tears fell across his scales and down across his tusk.

Azuran leapt into the air. The wind from his wings rustled through Crimson's fur and knocked her off-balance.

As the heat faded, Crimson reached for him until he disappeared. Like a flood, tears poured from her eyes. Crimson collapsed on the ground, shaking from the sobs.

"He needs time. Remember how you felt when you thought he had died. He feels that way now," Midnight said. "You did what you could. He has to heal in his own way. Maybe then he can rejoin dragon-kind."

Covelli moved up beside Crimson and pressed against her again, supporting her the only way she knew how. Comforting dragon magic surrounded her.

Crimson rubbed her nose between her paws, wiping away the moisture on her furry cheeks. She stood and stepped into the lake with Covelli. She let the water wash away her tears.

CHAPTER 24

CRIMSON watched Covelli swim in the lake. Months had passed since Crimson had seen Azuran. The scouts had reported no signs of the Schorl. Covelli had grown and Crimson had time to relax. There hadn't been any visitors in weeks, and Crimson took Covelli exploring. Covelli learned quickly and could navigate her way through the lake, even in darkness, without getting lost. They swam near the surface of the lake, and Covelli flapped her wings and jumped, gliding above the lake's surface. Then she was flying. Crimson cheered her on, even though, inside, her chest hurt and her stomach turned. Covelli would be leaving soon.

That night, Crimson slept restlessly.

Something moved. First it was like a shadow upon

the water; then it became a Norterridane. It was Jasper.

She walked out of the water, her body transparent and her fur swaying in the wind. She sat beside Crimson and looked across the mountain. There was a sadness surrounding Jasper. It was like a cloud of despair radiating from her fur.

"Open your eyes. The storm is coming."

The landscape changed before Crimson's eyes. It was no longer the peaceful lake of Genorrdia, but a dark forest of trees Crimson had never seen before. A dragon flew overhead, and out of the forest, strange creatures that walked on two legs came into view. Their furless bodies were draped with deer skin, and their eyes were large and black. They came through the forest like ants, their hands alive with magic, their eyes intent on killing.

Jasper looked down at Crimson with eyes full of terror.

"The storm is coming."

Crimson awoke with a jolt. What did the vision mean? What were those creatures? Cave-dwellers? They were similar to the hieroglyphs she had seen in the odd-shaped caves near the western ocean. Whatever those creatures were, they filled her with more dread than any thought of the serpents.

ONE DAY, when the leaves began to fall from the trees and the grasses browned, Covelli and Crimson swam through the lake to the river that poured into the lake from Mount Xenoti.

The river was deep at the beginning and slowly became shallower as they moved higher up the hills and into the mountain range. Small plants and rocks sprang up in the river, on the sides of small waterfalls where sediment had gathered. Covelli swam under the falling water and shook her body. Crimson stepped on stones and jumped to the riverbank. She sniffed the grasses. There were the scents of goats, deer, and algae. She smelled serpent, but it was old. Months old. There was also the scent of a dragon, more recent, but not for weeks. She had hoped to catch a glimpse of Azuran to say goodbye.

They returned to the lake to see Carnelian flying overhead. In her talons she carried Amber and Ferruginous. She landed and placed them on the lakeshore.

The Norterridane greeted and Ferruginous spoke. "Crimson, we have consulted with Hornblende, and we think it is in the best interest of all that you travel to Alannador when Covelli flies."

Crimson was speechless. She had always wondered what it would be like explore Alannador, but it never seemed a real possibility.

"There is a dragon there named Cinna. She can help you understand and control your power," Ferruginous said. "Alannador is a dangerous place. We are not ordering you to go, but asking."

"Has anyone heard anything about Azuran? Is he OK?" Crimson said.

"He is alive, but he is not ready to come," Carnelian said.

"Where is he?"

"Last I saw him, he was near the forest by Mount Xenoti. He visits the cliff ledge where the unhatched dragon died. He has many truths he needs to deal with."

"When do we leave?" Crimson said.

"We leave tomorrow."

"Tomorrow?" Crimson said. Tomorrow they would fly to Alannador. Was that what Jasper was warning her about? "I wanted to tell Amber that I saw Jasper. She … she came with a message."

"What message did she have?"

Crimson quickly explained what she had seen.

"Cave-dwellers. Perhaps Alannador will be more than you are bargaining for," Carnelian said.

"Or it is a message about the urgent need to seal the magic stone again," Ferruginous said. "This is our best hope."

"Did you hear the call?" she asked Covelli, and the young dragon flapped her wings enthusiastically.

Covelli was three times Crimson's size. Her beautiful turquoise wings glistened in the sun.

"I haven't had time to see Tourmaline," Crimson said, looking down at the ground.

"I will have her come tomorrow to say goodbye. I know this may seem sudden, but we need to secure this magic as soon as possible. If the serpents want the power, they will return."

"But Malachite is dead," Crimson said.

"Another leader always takes over. If there is one thing for certain, serpents will always crave magic. They will return," Carnelian said. Her wings were folded at her side, and Crimson saw the large scars across her leg. The serpents were getting stronger. What would this mean for the war?

"Carnelian will return tomorrow," Ferruginous said. He twitched his tail, and Carnelian wrapped her talons around him and Amber. They flew off toward the city.

WHEN DAWN ARRIVED, Crimson looked over Crystal Lake. The calm waters glistened in the morning sun, and Midnight was the first to arrive.

"I can't believe you're going to Alannador," Midnight said.

"I know. It's … it's exciting and scary all at the same time."

"The land of dragons. You can learn so much, see so much."

Crimson looked affectionately at Midnight. "And when I come back, you'd better be a pack leader."

"Yeah," Midnight said, pawing playfully at her.

Tourmaline came through the reeds and pressed her nose against Crimson's. "I had to come and see you off. Be safe and come back to me."

"I wish we had more time."

"When you come back, we will." Tourmaline said.

"I'm gonna miss you," Crimson said, pressing her head into her mom's soft white fur. She wished she could just go back to the Underground and be a pup again, at least for the moment.

Tourmaline gave her an affectionate lick on her muzzle.

Carnelian landed nearby. Crimson touched noses

with Midnight. Then Carnelian lifted Crimson up in her front claws and leapt from the lake into the air.

Midnight waved a paw in the air. Then they howled a goodbye.

The dragon flew into the air. A rush of wind blew across Crimson's face and through her fur. Covelli swam into the lake, swiftly speeding and then using her momentum to lift into the air. Crimson watched as she flew after them through the sky, as if she were swimming gracefully under water. The wind blowing in Crimson's face felt freeing, even as they passed the waterfall and the red willows. They were much too high to see the details. Crimson again thought of Azuran and prayed he would be OK.

They flew over trees, past the willows and the sand dunes. When they reached the western ocean, Covelli slowly flew down. She splashed into the water and swam under the ocean. Crimson called upon the dragon power, and felt the cool, breezy connection. Though she could no longer create gills, she felt safer knowing Covelli was close.

"Stay with me," she whispered. Carnelian's talons held her tight as they flew. Crimson's heart pounded. They were on their way to Alannador.

Thank you, for reading my novel. I hope you enjoyed the story and the characters.

Learn More

www.taimanivong.com